PAOLO

THE COUGARS AND CUBS SERIES 💋 BOOK #1

GIGI MEIER

GiGi Meier

Cover Design by GiGi Meier

Developmental Editing by Jessica Lessor

Editing by Robyne Hunt

Author Photograph by Tara L. Grundemeier

ISBN: 979-8-9877336-8-4 (e)

ISBN: 979-8-9877336-9-1 (pb)

GiGi Meier Media LLC

ALSO BY GIGI MEIER

Standalone Book

Coyote

Sammie and Carlos's forced proximity

cartel, kidnapped, Military hero, dark romance

The Cañon Series

Tomlin

The start of Dani and Tomlin's

slow burn, enemies-to-almost-lovers

Tomlin Takahashi Duet #1

The Cañon Series, Book #1

Takahashi

The conclusion of Dani and Tomlin's

friends-to-lovers, happily ever after

Tomlin Takahashi Duet #2

The Cañon Series, Book #2

Hamilton

Hamilton and Molli's second chance,

small town, police officer romance

The Cañon Series, Book #3

Isla

Gods and Goddesses Anthology

Eternal Reign

Hades and Persephone Modern Retelling

Russian bratva, kidnapping, touch her and die, slow burn.

GET A FREE BOOK

Sign up for my newsletter to ensure you are the first to know about new releases, sneak peek excerpts, cover reveals, book sales, and author giveaways!

The Cañon Series 🖤
is deliciously dark and intensely traumatic.

DOWNLOAD FOR FREE ON MY WEBSITE
www.gigimeier.com

Dani and Tomlin's story is a single POV, slow burn, enemies-to-lovers, forced proximity romance. Check my website for a list of content and trigger warnings.

DEDICATION

To dating younger, age is just a number.

PAOLO

1

TAYLOR

My fingers dance across the keyboard, basking in the afternoon glow that floods my corner office every Friday. The skyscrapers outside my window stand tall, silent sentinels guarding the bustling financial district below. This view used to fill me with pride, but now it's a constant reminder of the lifestyle that holds me captive.

Golden handcuffs are what they call it. Making too much money to walk away and with too much work to feel accomplished at anything.

The clock on my computer marches toward 5 pm. The echoes of colleagues granting well wishes for a joyous weekend fill the halls as they escape out the door to their family and home lives, leaving the corporate grind behind. It's another weekend, another trio of lonely nights in my high-rise apartment, a routine that's become all too familiar since my divorce a year ago.

The moment I opened that bedroom door and saw them entangled on our bed, my world tipped on its axis. My heart shattered into a million pieces, and the pain was excruciating. In the aftermath, I became a different person. I threw myself into my career with an intensity I had never known before, hoping my success would fill the void the betrayal left behind.

There are days when the questions still haunt me. How did I miss the signs? How could I have been so blind in the first place? The painful days are few and far between, but the loneliness is almost daily.

My phone buzzes, interrupting my thoughts. Glancing at the caller ID, I see it's Chloe, my best friend and colleague. I chuckle because she's probably still in the office too.

"Hey, Chloe."

"Taylor, I just heard Williamson's charging down the hall like a dark storm cloud," she whispers through the receiver. "He's looking for you."

By Williamson, she means Theodore R. Williamson III. Firstborn son and current Chairman of the Board of the expansive investment house that bears the moniker of his grandfather. Rarely is he on this floor. Even more rare is that he's looking for me.

My heart rate spikes as I furrow my brow.

"What for? He never talks to me, not directly, anyhow." He goes through my boss, the Chief Executive Officer, who's a stickler for following the chain of command and never stepping outside of it. When I glance across the glass offices, the CEO is already gone for the day, and his secretary is packing her bags to leave. "I'm buried with the quarterly filing due in two weeks."

Before I can continue complaining to her, Mr. Williamson bursts into my office. His usually impeccable gray hair is in disarray, and his face is a roadmap of bulging veins and angry red splotches.

"Taylor, just the person I wanted to see," he barks with an open collar and his tie hanging askew. "We've got a mess on our hands."

I replace the receiver in its cradle and gesture toward the guest chair on the other side of my desk.

"Please, have a seat."

Mr. Williamson remains standing, slamming a thick folder onto my desk. It hits with a resounding thud, startling me.

"This is Mr. Jacobsen's file, our most lucrative client. He's been with us for over a decade and is threatening to leave."

I blink at the name on the folder. Jacobsen & Associates has been a loyal client for years. They have an extensive real estate holdings company in addition to their oil drilling and mineral rights leases. I can't fathom why they'd want to cut ties now.

"What happened?"

"He's furious about some miscommunication regarding his portfolio. He's been trying to reach Jim all week about some recent trades he took the liberty of making into volatile international stocks, which directly conflicts with Mr. Jacobsen's risk tolerance. And now Jim isn't returning his calls." Mr. Williamson's voice drips with fury.

Fucking Jimothy.

Jimothy is what I call him. It's a disparaging nickname since he doesn't deserve the respect of being called by his proper name, Jim. The man is nearly twenty-five years older than me. He is a narcissistic egomaniac who regularly cheats on his wife with the country club beer cart girls. He broods about the office like he owns the place and treats me as if we are not equals when, in fact, we are. Something I remind my male chauvinistic boss of all the time since he continues to let Jimothy run amuck.

"I'm sorry to hear that, sir."

I'm not. I hope this is the straw that breaks the camel's back in getting him fired since the last three hostile work environment complaints against Jimothy haven't done the trick.

"I knew you would be. Since you're the only one of my senior executives still here, I will need you to get right on it. Familiarize yourself with his portfolio and trades, then be prepared to present your recommendations on Monday on how we save this relationship."

My stomach churns. My inbox is overflowing with emails, and my calendar is a cluster of back-to-back meetings. I don't have the time nor the inclination to handle this just because I'm still here on a Friday afternoon or to save Jimothy's ass yet again.

"Mr. Williamson. With all due respect, I'd love to help. As you know, I'll do anything for the good of the company. However, I have my accounts to handle, and I'm double booked with the quarterly filings due in two weeks. Perhaps another executive . . ." I crane my head to look back to the row of empty glass offices, knowing full well I'm the only one here. "Or perhaps Jim could come in this weekend and work on it. Since he's responsible—"

"Taylor, he's in Mexico on vacation with his wife."

"Oh."

I haven't had a vacation all year, prioritizing work over everything, even my well-being. Now I have to clean up the mess made by this rotten, scheming, and lazy bastard.

"It's settled then." He doesn't look pleased by my objection. That makes two of us. I'm not pleased either. "You'll present first so we can open it up to questions before proceeding with the regular agenda."

I hate Jimothy for this. And right now, I hate Mr. Williamson too. Mostly, I hate my loyalty to this company that goes unacknowledged and unrewarded.

"I'll get right on it and reach out to Mr. Jacobsen." I reach for my phone when his waving hand stops me.

"No need, I already did. Just see what you can find. Then we'll regroup before approaching the client."

He doesn't wait for my reply when he strides out of the office, leaving me alone to grapple with this situation. With an exasperated sigh, I pick up my phone and dial Chloe's number.

She's always the one I turn to when work becomes unbearable, especially since I got her the job here.

She picks up on the first ring. "What happened?"

I lean back in my chair, feeling the weight of the world suddenly on my shoulders.

"You won't believe the mess I'm in right now. Mr. Williamson just dropped this colossal problem on my desk. Jacobsen & Associates is about to jump ship because of some disaster with their portfolio. And guess who's responsible for this disaster?"

"Who?"

"Jimothy."

Chloe lets out an empathetic groan. "Jimothy again? That guy is a menace. I don't know how he keeps getting away with things around here."

I shake my head, my frustration mounting.

"You and me both. I've had it with his antics. The guy must have glossy pictures on someone here because nothing ever happens to him."

As I sift through the mess on my desk, I sigh into the phone.

"I hope this colossal blunder will be the final straw that leads to Jimothy's long-overdue termination from the company. Maybe, just maybe, it's time for him to face the consequences of his actions once and for all."

She grunts in disbelief. "I doubt it. Nothing ever happens to him. Not even when the Head of Human Resources filed a complaint. You know she left because of him."

"I didn't know that," I murmur, flipping open the client folder. "But right now, I must figure out how to salvage this relationship. I am going to have to work late tonight and all weekend to sort through this mess."

"Taylor, you're overworking yourself." Chloe's voice softens with sympathy. "This isn't healthy. When was the last time you went out and had a little fun?"

I can't remember.

"I don't even know, Chloe. It feels like forever. But I can't afford to drop the ball on this."

There's a brief pause on the line before she speaks again.

"I get it. Just promise me you'll take some time for yourself soon. We can plan a weekend getaway or something. Maybe get laid. Oh, wouldn't that be nice? To find two hot guys to wine and dine us, then drill me into the mattress."

I manage a faint smile. I can't remember the last time I had sex either. At least no one since the ex. That's absolutely something that needs to be rectified once I get past these deadlines.

"Yeah, a wild and carefree weekend is long overdue. I'd like that, but after this and after my quarterly filings." I sigh for the third time as if the exhalation will somehow change my reality. "Anyway, I need to order my dinner since security won't let anyone up after 6 pm."

"Okay, call me if you need me."

I put the receiver down, pull the folder closer, and begin poring over the documents.

Fucking Jimothy.

2

TAYLOR

The display cases are full of artistic pastries and look as delectable as they are colorful. It's the best marketing tactic this little bakery uses, judging by the number of fingerprints on the glass. I debate about sticking to my diet or blowing it entirely with a six-pack of macarons shimmering with sugar crystals and sprinkles.

To say everything in this place is over the top is an understatement, from the artisan desserts to the oven-fired crust on their five-cheese grilled sandwiches served with the best tomato basil soup I've ever tasted.

The place is filled with dewy-eyed couples staring at each other. Girlfriends hovering close to talk about last night's escapades. Families with their children spilling out of line and bumping into strangers. It's not the best place to work, but with the sun shining through the windows on this crisp autumn morning, it's the most entertaining.

As the line crawls toward the baristas, I spot a vacant four-seat table ideally situated out of the sun but near the window. If I can place my order in time, I can snag it and have plenty of space to sprawl out as I assemble my presentation for the Monday morning meeting.

Like the many fingerprints donning the glass, I point to those damn macarons knowing I shouldn't eat all of them but eventually will.

"A large pumpkin spice latte and a six-pack of the macarons."

Another marketing genius. The six-pack is considerably cheaper. If you consider twenty dollars for six cheap compared to five dollars per individual macaron. I'm a bargain shopper, or so I tell myself. My waistline would disagree.

After tapping my card on the machine and plucking my number from the counter, I book it to the table, barely beating out a little girl twirling in a pink tutu with some frosting smeared across her mouth and showing me her sticky fingers. Kids are adorable, so long as they are not mine. But this kid, with her sticky everything, is just dangerous as I glance at my new Hermes tweed skirt and perfectly matching boots.

Luckily, someone across the bakery calls her name, and she twirls away, putting my skirt safely out of the danger zone. I pull out the chair closest to me to dump my laptop bag and purse on it before shoving my card in my wallet and digging for my phone. No new messages, which is a blessing as I have several hours' worth of work.

Next is my laptop, power cord, and notes—everything I need to dive in and get started. Once my mini command center is set up, I plop in my chair and start working. The presentation isn't as complicated as I thought, just tedious, with a lot of bad news about Jimothy's suspicious trading activity at our client's expense.

Time goes by before a shadow looms over me. I assume it's the barista bringing my sweet treats and latte, something I needed five slides ago. It's not.

It's a tall brunette with hair too long to work a corporate

job, glancing around and looking for a spot to sit. His crossbody laptop bag sits against his hip, pulling his button-down shirt snugly against his defined chest. His rolled-up sleeves speak to the casualness of the day, as do his crisp khaki pants and boat shoes. When he runs a hand through his thick chocolate hair, I spot the stack of friendship bracelets wound around his wrist. It catches me off guard.

Back when I was growing up, only girls made and wore them. Symbols of their strong BFF ties when they matched down to the black and white letters that stated "BFF." His bracelets don't say that. They have little ocean charms on them, causing me to think he's probably an activist of some sort. It would explain the long hair and countless hours spent at the gym working out by the looks of his high, tight ass.

The second his arm drops and his head turns my way, I'm busted for checking him out. What I don't expect is how freaking young he is. Damn, I'm a cradle robber, fantasizing about a kid that probably just left his parent's house to work on his high school assignment. Why did he have to be so good looking? Shouldn't he have pimples or something? I know I did well into my thirties, and this kid shows up with luxurious hair and flawless skin. Life's a real kick in the ass sometimes.

I quickly duck my head, my cheeks ablaze with embarrassment for analyzing him like fresh meat in this super family-friendly place. My attempts to appear overly engrossed in my slide deck fail when he levels his bulging package on the table's edge.

Well, not bulging as if he whipped it out and sat his nuts on the table but pretty damn close, judging how it strains against the fabric of his tight pants. An example of spectacular advertising on his part. I wonder how many dates he wears those pants on that result in him getting laid.

I can't even go there with him. I'm already horrified that I was sizing him up. Now I'm thinking about him having sex. It couldn't get any worse.

"Excuse me, ma'am?"

Ma'am.

It's what I call old people as a sign of respect. His calling me that now means I'm old to him. That's a shame.

His voice is sexy, rumbling out of that accomplished chest through the airwaves and into my welcoming ears. With nowhere to hide, I tuck my hair behind my ear to act casual when I look at him, appearing to notice him for the first time.

"Yes?"

I keep my voice light and airy, knowing I'm too damn old to think what I'm thinking about him. Plus, men can't be trusted. My ex proved that perfectly. Hot, young men like him doubly can't be trusted.

He has the darkest brown eyes I have ever seen, simultaneously looking into and past me. How did the universe know I'm a sucker for brunettes with dark brown eyes?

"Would you mind if I share your table? There seems to be nowhere else to sit."

I detect a slight accent on certain words but can't make it out exactly. He makes it a point to look around the crowded bakery, which is unnecessary. I know. I selfishly took a larger table and could have easily waited for a two-seat table to vacate, but I wanted to spread out and get this presentation done.

"Of course," I say, motioning to the chair diagonal from me when he gives me the sweetest smile.

He has a mustache dusting his upper lip and a sprinkling of a beard. Too young to grow a full one is probably what is happening here. His front teeth are slightly larger than the rest but otherwise straight and bright white. His grin comes fast and easy. Too damn easy to be looking at someone like me the way he is right now.

I scoot my chair back and stand, packing up some of the stuff I scattered across the table when I notice how tall he is. Easily taller than my five-foot-eight frame and yet another thing I shouldn't concern myself with. He's a kid—a baby. I probably could have given birth to him and not have been a teenage mom. Think of him as my possible child, and my lust will disappear.

He waits patiently as I stack everything on my side of the table, leaving the other side to him. He fastens his order number to my silver table flag. Both numbers are together. As in touching each other, and I blow out a quick breath. Being this attracted to a kid is stupid and something I won't entertain anymore.

Cool it, Taylor.

"There you go," I announce for no reason but to release some discomfort. That gets me another easy smile, and I hustle into my chair to get super engrossed in my slides. When did it get so hot in here? I haven't even had my coffee yet, and I'm already sweating in my cable-knit sweater.

He carefully sets up his laptop, takes cautious steps not to disturb me, and whispers, "Sorry," when his leg bumps into the table. I don't bother with a reply. I let my smile say it all, which he returns with one of his own.

Several minutes pass of me stealing glances as he sits diagonally from me, dragging a notebook from his bag, a pen, and a pencil to set beside his laptop. He glances at his watch, frowns, and then starts working.

Another shadow falls on us. This time, it is who I've been expecting. The barista announces my order and looks from him to me before setting my latte and six-pack of macarons down behind his laptop. The employee snatches up my number and tells him that his tea should be out in a few moments, but he's too busy peeking over the edge of his screen and greedily eyeing the colorful macarons.

I can't stop myself from blurting out, "Have one if you'd like."

It comes after his third glance over his screen, and I get a guilty grin this time.

"Do you mind? They are my favorite and were sold out when I asked."

Stinking cute is what he is. That accent hitting on every third word, the shyness in his smile, and the timid way he reaches over his laptop to pluck the shimmery blue one sends me over the edge. He doesn't bother with a napkin, and when it crumbles like the finely crafted air pastry it is all over his keyboard, he cusses under his breath. I chuckle and hand him a few of the napkins I snaked while waiting in the long line for the barista to take my order.

"Thanks."

I nod, take the pink confetti one, and place it on my napkin to break into pieces before plopping one in my mouth. His macaron is gone in a flash, and when our eyes meet, he has blue shimmery dust across his lips. My gaze darts from those perfect lips to his dark eyes reflecting the sun behind me and back down to where his tongue darts out to lick the shimmer away.

Holy fuck.

Either he knows what he's doing, or he knows what he's doing. A wicked smile pulls up on his face, and I look down at my drink before clearing my throat. Okay, I'm not the only one feeling it.

"I'm Paolo, by the way," he says, the accent hitting the vowels just right and sending a bolt of heat between my legs.

Paolo.

Is it just me, or is it how it rolls off his tongue that has me thinking of tongues and all the wonderful things they can do? Does he have an accent when he groans in pleasure? Or does it go away like singers of other countries do when covering American songs? Either way, I'd love to know.

Paolo.

Of course, he's Italian. They are the best at everything—cars, food, fashion, wine, models, and accomplished lovers. But this Italian is young. Younger than my forties by the looks of his creaseless forehead and bag-free under eyes. Younger than the Hermes bag I inherited from my mother that sits next to me in the chair.

His hand lingers in the air across the table. When I slip my hand into his, it's warm and inviting. His long fingers curl over mine in a firm grip, not shaking it but more holding it in place. My brain can't stop thinking about his age compared to my age. It's got to be two decades at least, or else he has some amazing skincare products that I need to use.

"Nice to meet you, Paolo."

When I say it, it doesn't ooze sex appeal like his way of saying it. It sounds like plain old American, and suddenly, I don't want to hold hands in the air across the table.

"Help yourself to another macaron. I can't eat them all."

I can, and I would, but not with this young Italian stud sitting across from me. I untangle my hand from his, ignoring his reluctance to let go and grab my cup to hide my face.

"And your name?" he asks, snatching up another shimmery one. I'm onto him this time.

I answer his question and feign interest in something out the window, not to watch him lick his lips while wondering how skilled his tongue is at licking other things.

His tea arrives just in time for me to steal a glance and see no shimmer on his lips. He's engrossed in chatting with the barista. I take full advantage of the opportunity to dive back into my presentation, knowing I need to finish it at lightning speed and get the hell out of here. Otherwise, I might end up chatting him up, inviting him to my place, and having that wild weekend Chloe mentioned yesterday.

It's been too damn long since I've had fantastic sex, and sitting across from this Italian stud is not helping the situation. Their conversation continues for a while, allowing me enough time to focus. I get another five slides done, flipping in and out of different windows to collect the information I need when the barista leaves.

The longer he sits with me, the more fixated I become on his movements. The way he gently sips his tea. He smiles at the people walking by when they catch him deep in thought. The way he nibbles at the pencil in his mouth while he types. If he has an oral fixation, I suddenly do too.

The age bothers me. It shouldn't, though. How many old geezers at work are chasing skirts and have young mistresses? Plenty. So, what if the roles are reversed? It's the twenty-first century, for crying out loud. If I wanted a go at a younger one, so be it. Plenty of women are into younger guys.

Cubs, they call them. If this kid is a cub, then that makes me a cougar. A term I've never applied to myself before and am not entirely comfortable with now, but I see the appeal if this is how it starts. If, by happenstance, I must share a table at a crowded little corner bakery to work, and the universe plants a gorgeous, young, athletic Italian at my table, what's a cougar to do? I mean a woman. What's a woman to do? Stop dwelling on his age and youthful appearance and start appreciating the glances he keeps stealing at me.

My elbows stick to the tabletop as I lean closer to my laptop. As if he's been waiting for this moment, he mimics my actions with a tilt of his head. The bracelets slide down his arm as he repeatedly sweeps his unruly hair behind his ear.

"You're a very beautiful woman. Very intriguing."

His words are liquid sex appeal, even if they are a bunch of lies. I'm fifteen pounds heavier, thanks to the pandemic. I wear patches under my eyes to reduce puffiness after my shower and sometimes wear reading glasses on weary nights staring at the computer. My hair doesn't grow as fast anymore, and my nails stop growing after years of wearing fake ones. I'm not an Instagram model worthy. Those years passed along with my youth.

"You're too kind, Paolo. But—" I stop, unwilling to spill all my flaws to this perfectly flawless Italian with a slight macaron obsession. "Never mind."

"It is the truth. In my country, there is beauty in wisdom. Knowledge in experience. And an appreciation for older women."

Either Paolo is hitting on me, or Paolo is hitting on me. I can't say this happens really at all, ever. To say I'm taken back is an understatement, even if I'm hugely flattered.

"Are you from Italy?" I ask, assuming he is, or else I'm wrong for referring to him as an Italian stud in my mind.

"Yes, my family is from Milan. Are you familiar with it? Have you been?"

He snaps the lid of his laptop shut and shoves his chair closer to the table, bringing him within arm's reach. Both are unnecessary since my presentation is incomplete, and I need to work, but answering a few questions won't hurt.

"No, I have not. I want to go, though," I answer honestly this time.

"*Mia cara,* it's everything. Milan is magnificent. The museums and artists are superb, with new art installations to tour. The food is exquisite, fresh from the country, and not the processed food you have here. And the architecture is centuries old and steeped in culture."

His face softens when he talks of his homeland, and his voice grows almost reverent. I notice the tug of homesickness in his eyes and wonder why he chose to leave.

"Are you here visiting then? On vacation."

I save my work before closing my laptop. I'll finish the rest at home, over a glass of red wine and some cold pizza, not very Italian-like. His eyes spark at my actions, and he leans further into the table, putting his elbows in the center and almost touching me.

"No, I live here. It's a long story. One I'd love to tell you over dinner."

Smooth. Very smooth.

I lean away from him, my chair creaking as I put space between us. His expression is unreadable as he slowly breaks our gaze. Neither speaks for what feels like an eternity, the air tense and heavy around us.

"I'm older than you."

His face lights up. The corners of his lips curl into a playful smirk, and his eyes shift from dark to light again. His expression suggests he's relishing a challenge, although I'm unsure why.

"Yes, I know."

"Way older."

"You don't look *way older*."

His accent is thick and exotic when emphasizing my words, and now I am frowning. He could read me the dictionary, and I'd cream my panties like I'm doing now.

"Trust me, I am."

"If you say so," he concedes with a shrug. "How about dinner? I know of this terrific little place close to here. Small and intimate."

He's undeterred. I've got to give him props for that. If the roles were reversed, I'd be packing my bags right now from being rejected.

"Hold on. How old are you? Have you gone to dinner with someone my age before? Someone *way older* than you?"

I narrow my eyes so he understands I'm onto him. I know he's looking for a booty call. Maybe I am too, but subtly is not my forte. If we're going to do this, I want all the cards on the table. I don't like surprises like he's a serial killer who escaped from Italy or lives in a frat house on campus. Or worse, he's unemployed and can't pay for said dinner.

"And a few other things. Do you live with your parents? Do you have a job? Do you have a criminal record? Are you married or have someone that thinks you're in a relationship with?"

I rack my brain, remembering all the red flags I've learned from Chloe's dating fiascos to ask him. He laughs, and it's as sexy and smokey as whiskey with a cigar.

"I love the directness of women your age. Cut straight to the chase," he says after he composes himself. Men are liars. It's my job to flush them out and turn on them.

"And?" I wave a hand in the air, prompting him to answer.

"I'll be twenty-five in March. And yes, I have dated older women. Not—"

Twenty-four years old.

I could've been a teenage mom. Could've given birth to him. The thought is offputting.

"Why?" I cut him off. We'll get to the rest in a minute.

He switches chairs so he's directly across the table from me. Our knees brush, sending a jolt of electricity through my body, and I sit up to avoid that happening again. He moves the vase with the fresh flowers hindering his view to the empty macaron plate.

"More intelligent, more engaging, and deeper conversations."

"Fair. But we don't have the hot, firm bodies to match this?" Again, I wave a hand at him because, seriously, if we were to have sex, it might need to be in the dark. "Some of us have cellulite and stretch marks."

"Then you are a woman that looks like a woman should."

His response is fast but not rehearsed, and his brown eyes sparkle with sincerity.

17

GIGI MEIER

"And to answer your other questions, yes, I am employed, and no to the other three."

I honestly can't remember the other three. When he leans forward, I can feel his closeness, like an invisible tether is forming between us.

"Come to dinner with me tonight. You can decide from there where it goes."

I know where it will go. I'll drink a glass of wine, maybe two, and then all inhibitions will go out the window. The night will end before it begins with me asking about his place or mine. I don't need to go to dinner to know that once my car pulls into the restaurant parking lot, it will be game over for me, and hoping he has condoms.

"I know where it will go, and I'm not going there."

"Why not? I want to get to know you more. You intrigue me." His fingers are lightly intertwined, and he seems perfectly content with having this conversation in the middle of this busy bakery. "I believe I intrigue you too."

"Maybe."

Not that I'm looking to date or be in a relationship. Far from it. He's probably far from it too. It could be a one-night stand for each of us. Scratch an itch or explore a curiosity—something like that.

He reaches into his pocket, pulls out his phone, and places it on the table. Then, with a subtle gesture, he slides it toward me, his eyes locking onto mine in anticipation.

"Put your number in there."

Bold move.

"Why?"

"I don't want you to slip away."

My gaze sweeps over him, noting the tousled waves of his hair as it untucks from his ear and drapes like a curtain down one side of his face. His eyes are liquid chocolate from the intensity of his stare, melting my insides. He's unflustered by my penetrating look.

"How many times have you used this move on a woman?"

I have got to give it to him. It's hot, cocky, and confident. I'm not sure what they teach these kids nowadays in school, but guys my age don't have half this amount of confidence. His unshakeable determination intrigues me, as do other things. I find myself sucked into this back and forth, push and pull between us. He's giving as good as he's taking. Most guys at the office have fragile male egos, and this kid has self-esteem for days.

"Once. She's giving me a hard time about it. Now put it in."

That last sentence sends visions of me saying the same thing to him. Damn, this guy. It'd be my first time with a younger man, but what the hell, I only live once. I smile, pick up his phone, and enter my name, followed by the word cougar.

"Happy now?"

I slide his phone back to him, which he snatches up and tucks into his pocket.

"Very."

He must have dropped his voice or infused more accent onto that little word because I'm ready to crawl across this tiny table and see where it goes.

"I'll text you the address. See you at 7 pm."

"I didn't say I was going. I merely gave you my number."

"You'll go. You're as interested as I am. Oh, and wear a skirt."

"A skirt?"

His brown eyes smolder with raw, carnal desire. Dark pools of lust are hidden behind a curtain of lashes. My body is flush with an energy current coursing through my veins. The anticipation of the night ahead causes me to squirm in my seat, and I can't help but wonder how far he'll take this. The dinner date is only the beginning, a tiny spark igniting into a roaring flame that will lead to closed bedrooms, whispered conversations, and pleas for more.

"Please."

His voice is low, husky, and full of promise. The way he says 'please' makes me shiver with excitement. I can't believe I'm agreeing to this, but something about him makes me feel desirable and wanted despite the divorce, the pandemic weight gain, and the cellulite. The taboo of it is alluring. Even with the flutter of butterflies in my stomach, I know I can always say no at the restaurant. Or I can have one night I'll never forget.

"Okay," I whisper, my voice barely audible. "I'll wear a skirt."

3

PAOLO

"**M**atch!"

It's another triumph in a day that's already been surprisingly excellent. First, the chance encounter with that alluring woman at the café and now, the sweet satisfaction of beating him on his own court.

"Stop gloating," Sebastian retorts with a playful grin, his competitive spirit clear. "I let you have that one, and you know it."

He hops over the net, extending his hand for a handshake that quickly turns into a jostling hug. His racket bumps my leg while his arm hangs from my neck.

"You have yet to beat me. Not back home or here."

I tug at the headband, drenched with sweat and move it into my hairline.

"Whatever," he chuckles, his arm sliding comfortably around my shoulders. "Let's go grab a beer."

"What about all this?"

I point my racket to a collection of tennis balls clustered in the corners of the court. He waves a dismissive hand so as not to be bothered with them.

"Somebody will get them."

Somebody is any member of his staff that runs this estate. His parents tragically perished in a private airplane crash that my parents narrowly escaped being on when my mother fell ill and couldn't board the flight. My parents step in as his surrogate family when he needs their assistance. Yet, his immense wealth means he rarely does.

"Doesn't it get tiring having people pick up after you? Waiting on you hand and foot?"

Even though my family has generational wealth and an estate back home, I prefer to live alone. Having staff always around makes me uneasy, but Sebastian doesn't seem to mind. He has always enjoyed this extravagant lifestyle.

"Doesn't it get tiring, you asking?"

With a light laugh, he releases his hold on my shoulders, moving swiftly to unlatch the gate leading out of the court. With an agile jog, he takes the steps two at a time past the stadium seating and up to the nearby pavilion.

"And I don't see you stopping to shag balls."

"Touché."

I cast him a guilty look and admittedly enjoy this privilege more than I should.

His property is vast and in the heart of the city. It boasts a pavilion with outdoor seating for a hundred people with echoes from past charitable events held under the outdoor chandeliers. Gondola rides in the largest residential swimming pool in the city was a novelty, and photos adorned the local society papers. Glitzy parties, charity tennis matches, and heads of state dinners are haunted ghosts of this luxurious estate. It's got to be lonely living here alone—vastly different from my cozy bungalow.

"Your serves were coming in hot. What gives?" he says, standing at the top of the landing and looking over the land that bears his family name and crest.

"I've got a date tonight."

I'm not entirely sure why I let that slip. It seemed unlikely she'd type her number into my phone. But when I texted her, and she responded immediately, my heart leaped with surprise and excitement. She didn't give me a fake number. She even called herself a cougar in the contacts, which makes me smile. Something I might not share with Sebastian. He'd rib me for days about having a *cougar* girlfriend. Something he did with the last older woman I dated.

"Seriously?"

He eases into an armchair beneath the gentle rotation of a ceiling fan in one of the cabanas flanking the sides of the dual sweeping staircases. I gesture toward the outdoor fridge, and he raises two fingers, signaling his desire for a beer. The chill feels good in my sweaty hands when I retrieve the bottles, and I refrain from pressing it against my heated forehead. I doff the caps on the mounted bottle opener and hand him a bottle.

"Yes."

Her smile came quickly when I asked to sit with her. The skepticism that followed, well, that was harder and not what I expected. Older women are always challenging and usually fall into three categories. Disgusted and outraged. Flattered and surprised. Open and eager. Taylor didn't really fall into any of them. She was a blend of all three. Maybe not disgusted or outraged, but more cynical and suspicious. Her questioning me was proof of that.

"You haven't been out in a long time. What gives?"

As he takes a sip of his beer, he absentmindedly twirls the end of his racket on the arm of the chair. Meanwhile, I place my racket on the table and settle beside him to enjoy the autumn breeze with my refreshing drink.

I shake my head. "Nothing gives. Unlike others, I'm particular about who I spend my time with."

His smirk is quick, a testament to the parade of girls vying for his attention when they see what he drives or learn where he lives. Neither seems to bother him as it would me.

"Alright, I'll bite. What is so particular about this one? She got big cans or a fat ass?"

Annoyed that he reduces women to body parts, I counter with the obvious.

"She's older."

He chuckles while his expensive racket clatters to the stone patio.

"Paolo, my man. You have got to be kidding me. I thought you gave all that up when the last one dumped you for being too young?"

His question, while laced with jest, strikes a chord. It's a reminder of my past and the challenges that come with age differences in relationships. She didn't exactly 'dump me.' She was promoted to their head offices in New York, which took her out of state, and she didn't ask me to accompany her. I was completing my master's degree, but I could have joined her afterward if only she had wanted the same.

In hindsight, the age difference bothered her more than I realized. It came up in little things, such as not allowing me to attend colleague dinners or the company holiday party. I used to laugh it off, but it actually hurt my feelings. It's why I'm not ready to dive into anything serious right now. I prefer older women, and having a little fun with Taylor fills that void, even if it's only temporary.

Deciding it's not worth correcting him about my break-up, I continue, "Well, this one's different. She's truly stunning. She has these captivating dark green eyes that narrow in concentration and light up when genuinely amused."

"Eyes? Don't be a pussy. Tell me about her body. Is it rocking?"

I ignore his vulgar language, something my upbringing frowns upon.

"Seb, be respectful."

"Sorry, bro. I'll stop." He takes a long drink, gazing out on the afternoon sun and allowing me some peace before starting up again. "Okay, you've got to give me something. Eyes just aren't cutting it."

"Her cheeks flushed when she was gazing at my lips," I relent, balancing my drink on the edge of the chair as he leans forward.

"Now we're getting somewhere." He finishes his beer, puts the empty bottle on the table, and rubs his hands together.

"I think she's as interested in me as I am in her."

I take a drink, letting my mind wander to the memory of her hunching over her computer, appearing busy when I turned to face her. Unbeknownst to her, I studied her while I stood in line, having noticed her long before she caught sight of me.

"Okay, but is she hot?"

"She's sexy and curvy."

I chuckle, thinking about her eyebrows pinching together when she asked me about cellulite and stretch marks as if such things bothered me. If she only knew how hard I was under the table as I envisioned her bent over with me taking her from behind. The thought is making me hard now and I shift in my chair to calm down.

"I love curvy chicks. All that flesh to hold on to."

He falls back into his chair with a satisfied sigh. Moment ticks by with each of us lost in our thoughts. Mine of her. Sebastian's of who knows.

"Hey, what about the new gig?"

His preference for American slang humors me.

"My new job, you mean?"

"Gig, job, whatever."

"I start my assignment on Monday."

"Assignment? Sounds like spy stuff. Isn't your degree in accounting or finance?"

I smile. Sebastian couldn't care less about my academic degrees, but it is intriguing to see him attempting to recall them.

"Forensic accounting. Basically, some abnormalities have been detected. My father can't seem to get straight answers as a board member. He convinced the chairman to hire me as an independent consultant."

He emits an uninterested hum, so I keep the details of my assignment brief.

"Didn't you do something like this before? Like go in and bust people for embezzling?"

"Undisclosed insider trading and contractual kickbacks. Yes, something similar."

"Well, go get them, tiger."

He makes a scratching paw motion in the air when he fakes a roar. I roll my eyes at his nonsense.

The breeze picks up as the sun dips lower in the sky, sending a golden hue over the treetops and across his two pools. The big one has a fountain in the center that could compete for the water show at the Bellagio. It's a shame this place doesn't see the festivities it once did.

"Do you remember when you pissed in the pool during that party, and your parents took the Porsche away?"

I press the bottle to my lips and sip as he looks at the grotto across the expansive patio.

"It was right before Santa Claus arrived with the firefighters to collect the gifts for that children's charity," he says, picking at something on the arm of his chair.

I used to avoid talking about his parents until he told me he liked to reminisce occasionally as I'm his only friend from the old country. All his friends here in Houston are new and never knew his parents.

"I was so blitzed. The only thing I remember about that night is making out with the dog in the catering kitchen."

He chuckles, smile lines cutting on both sides of his face when he looks at me. That night was the best and last party they ever had. Shortly after, they died en route to Italy. The sudden loss aged him overnight. He looks years older than me even though we are the same age.

"Your father was so angry that his face was beat red, and your mother had to warn him about his heart. He called for Jiles to collect you after you shoved me in the pool," I continue as we stare at the spot where it occurred.

"Good old Jiles. He's around here somewhere." He twists in his chair as if looking for him, knowing he wouldn't be intrusive enough to approach unless called for. "Man, I miss those days."

A deep sigh loosens from his body when he settles back in his chair. His expression is familiar. The unfairness of life gave him all this when he would easily trade it for his parents being alive and well. I finish my beer, place it on the table, and tap his leg.

"Why don't you have something like that now? Maybe not as grand and glitzy as they did. Probably not boat rides in the pool, but some event for the kid's charity again. You could do with blowing the dust off this place."

It's a precarious position that I put him in, suggesting he host a charity gala as his parents always did. It could be just the thing to pull him out of his aimless life. Or it could sink him into depression—both equal possibilities.

Yet, he needs something to focus on besides himself and having a good time. Without a job or degree, his days are spent wandering these lonely rooms or chasing half-naked women around his bedroom suite. His escapades are widely known amongst the staff. It wouldn't surprise me if they had to sign non-disclosure agreements to work here.

"Why? You want to bring your new sexy woman to my place to show her off?"

He stands, grabs another beer, and motions at me to ask if I want another, which I decline.

Would I bring her to his Christmas party?

December is two months away. That's more permanent relationship type of stuff than casual dating. Although I'm reluctant to confess nursing a heartbreak and bruised ego to him, I opt for the easier route and agree with him.

"If you have a holiday party and things work out with her, yes. I'll bring her."

I may be overplaying my hand. When she licked her lips today, all I could think about was her licking my cock. I had to move in closer. I had to see if she was as affected by me as I was by her.

"When are you seeing her again?"

Sebastian collapses in his chair, consuming almost half the bottle in one gulp before nonchalantly propping his feet onto the table. He knocks over the empty bottle, which he dismisses with a casual wave, knowing that *someone* will handle the cleanup.

"Tonight." I flick my wrist. The time on my watch has me jumping out of my seat. "Actually, I've got to go. I'm running late as it is."

He arches a sarcastic eyebrow.

"The great Paolo, running late? She must be pretty special to get you running around like a dog."

I chuckle again, unwilling to let his comment affect my jovial mood.

"Let's just say I've got a promising evening ahead of me."

Sebastian offers me a knowing smirk. "Ah, I see. Well, don't let me keep you. Go have your fun."

I flash him a grin as I grab my tennis bag and racket cover.

"Thanks for the match and drinks. We'll catch up soon." I

leave the cabana and then turn to shout, "And Seb, consider that Christmas party idea. It wouldn't hurt to have something to keep you occupied."

He gives me a nonchalant wave, focusing on finishing his beer. My thoughts quickly turn to her as I jog up the staircase to the terrace and the front door beyond. I retrieve my phone to text her the restaurant's address and a message expressing my excitement for the evening ahead. When she says she's looking forward to it, I smile brighter.

4

TAYLOR

The restaurant is dark, with low ceilings and candles on tables covered with crisp white linens. A bank of maroon leather booths is on the far end, with a single ceiling spotlight casting a golden hue over the patrons at each table. On the opposite end is a wall lined with bottles of exotic alcohol and dominated by a long, polished hardwood countertop. At the end of the bar is a service window where a man with a towel over his shoulder leans on his forearms, talking to the bartender.

Paolo and I traded several flirty texts leading up to this date. The constant pinging of my phone left me little time to prepare. It also added to my guilt of failing to complete my presentation to my usual high standards before I came. Every thought in my head battled each other, from wanting to cancel on him and finish my work to wanting to give in to a night of fun and passion. I debated all afternoon and finally talked to Chloe. Her insistent but unnecessary 'take a break from work and get laid' encouragement is how I find myself here.

If small means intimate, then Paolo is right. The place is too dark to be anything but a precursor to hook-up sex. Or, basically, the whole reason I came.

"Taylor," he purrs, my name coming through the door.

It's my new favorite way of pronouncing it. He stoops to kiss my cheek, a bold move that burns my skin. His gaze is magnetic, and he takes particular pleasure in assessing me from head to toe. A thrill runs through me at being the subject of such desire.

"You look even more beautiful than before."

I don't. Other than I changed into a two-piece dress that shows more skin than my Hermes outfit at the bakery. His dark sports coat, pressed slacks, and gleaming dress shoes match the restaurant's low lighting and heavy black velvet curtains, all designed for a special night out. His long hair is slicked back, and his fresh cologne adds to his overall handsome appearance.

"You're not so bad yourself."

He smiles, the corners of his eyes crinkling, as he offers his arm in invitation.

"We'll seat ourselves. I called ahead to secure us the best table in the house."

His footsteps echo on the marble floor as he leads me past clusters of well-dressed patrons to a secluded booth in the corner. If by 'best' he means private, then we definitely got the crème de la crème of seating arrangements. The booth is positioned perfectly to survey the entire room without drawing unwanted attention—a clever vantage point.

Surrounding us are walls crafted from polished walnut, each plank gleaming under the warm glow thrown by wall-mounted sconces. Heavy drapes flank the sides of the secret alcove, adding to the allure. I inhale deeply, taking in the musky scent of wood varnish that clings to the surface of this place.

He's quick to move my hand into his as I shimmy onto the

edge of the seat. When I release his hand to continue toward the middle, his fingertips graze my shoulder, making me aware of my dress breaking from my skin. All these subtle touches tantalize the fire brewing within me.

Once he's seated, a maître-d appears from the shadows with a wine list. Given the dark lighting and weary eyes from my presentation, I can't make out a thing on the list. I don't need to when Paolo and the man go back and forth in Italian before he nods and glides away.

"I ordered wine and a few hors d'oeuvres. Nothing too heavy."

Nothing too heavy.

I understand completely. Sex on a full stomach is revolting. As for the wine? I feel there will be a lot of wine on this date.

"You spoke so beautifully," I compliment, leaning slightly toward him, which doesn't go unnoticed.

Paolo's eyes are deep pools of molten chocolate, his long eyelashes fanning when he blinks. How he looks at me is better than any of the beautifully accented words that fall from his pillow lips.

"Very skilled," I add when he says nothing.

He closes the small distance between us, his face moving into my hair and whispering, "You have no idea."

My chin lowers as I angle my face toward him. His cologne swirls into my senses. His lips brush the sensitive skin on my neck, sending ripples of desire over my body.

"I'm skilled at a great many things, mia cara."

I take a deep breath and close my eyes, savoring the sweetness of his lips and the warmth of his breath on my skin. He could be my server, a colleague's son, or a neighborhood kid.

Yet here I am with a man almost half my age, and he's making me feel like the most desirable woman in the room. I shiver as his lips caress down my neck and onto my exposed shoulder before leaving my heated skin.

"I'm glad you came," he whispers, snapping me out of my trance, his eyes fixed on mine. I'm unsure what to say, but I can't break our gaze. My defenses have melted away, and I'm getting lost in my desire for him.

"I'm glad I came too," I murmur, leaning in to capture those lips with my own. He evades me, teasing me with a smile while draping an arm over the back of the booth.

"I have a little confession."

"Oh, what is that?" I bite my lip.

"I can't stop thinking about you."

His dark eyes spark with energy as they examine every inch of my body before finally meeting my gaze with a mischievous smile.

"Can't stop thinking about what?" I tease, knowing it's the same as what I have been thinking about ever since he called me ma'am and asked to sit at my table.

"I'd like to have dinner with you. Then, if you'd let me, I'd like to take you home and fuck you until you can't see straight."

Bold.

The same boldness of pushing his phone at me and kissing my cheek at the door. Not that I haven't had vulgar things said to me before. I have, and I usually hate it. But this . . . this is bold, blunt, and cocky and a straight shot to my pussy.

I try to blink away the blush, but I can't hide the subtle smile that tugs at the corners of my mouth when he inches nearer to kiss me. His lips are warm. His tongue is sweet and soft, wrapping around mine and coaxing it to play with his. His hand cradles my neck, encouraging me closer until our bodies press together, and I feel his hard muscles beneath the fabric of his clothing.

His fingertips stroke a lazy line up my thigh, pushing my hem high enough not to be proper and so far away from where I want it to go. My breath quickens as my pussy tingles. His playful fingers coax goosebumps to the surface as I melt further

33

into his arms. It's hot, new, exciting, and forbidden. I can't get enough.

The chemistry between us is unbelievable, leaving me curious about what sex would be like with him. Hopefully, hours and hours of it until I'm tired, sore, and completely sated.

I don't even hear the maître-d coming back bearing a silver tray laden with food and wine until Paolo makes excuses. I straighten up, embarrassed and avert my eyes. With decorum, the man quickly arranges everything on the table and immediately excuses himself.

"We got carried away."

"Yes, we did."

He steals a kiss, and then another and another until I'm pushing against the buttons of his dress shirt to stop him. The minty flavor of his mouthwash lingers on my lips, leaving them tingling and feeling fresh.

"Can you pour the wine?" I ask, wanting to keep his hands busy with something other than me.

"Of course."

He steals a final kiss before releasing me to handle the task. I run a hand over my hair, winding a stray strand into my low bun from where his fingers caught in it and taking a moment to compose myself.

He fills my glass with the burgundy liquid that smells of wood and spice before setting a plate between us, intending for us to share. With a flick of his wrist, he plucks the silver dome from the platter of hors d'oeuvres, where four distinct selections await us.

"I hope you're hungry," Paolo says, reaching for the spoon to place a few sautéed shrimp on the plate. I smile when he stabs a prawn with his fork and moves it toward my lips. Never has someone fed me before, and it feels intimate and sexy.

"Unless there's something else on your mind."

The smell of the food is irresistible, and he dares me to say what I want while gently seducing my senses with this savory aroma. I slowly wrap my lips around the dripping prawn, sucking it from his fork as a little precursor to tasting him later tonight. When the sauce catches on my lips, I slowly glide my tongue across them under his lustful stare.

"Not really," I say, playing coy.

His lips move gracefully as he whispers, "You'll have to excuse me if I don't believe you."

Our eyes remain locked, and the rising heat thickens the tension.

"Are you calling me a liar?" I challenge, reaching for my wine and letting it partially hide my face.

He lets out a deep, husky chuckle.

"I believe you to be many things, but a liar doesn't seem to be one of them."

He pushes the sautéed shrimp around on the plate, gazing at me and leaving me wondering how long I can keep up this seduction game before I finally give in.

"How do you know what I am? We only just met."

And yet, I've had his tongue in my mouth already. I push that morally true statement from my mind to settle back into the seductress I want to be.

"I know you're smart and ambitious if you work on a Saturday. I know you're beautiful, and keeping my hands off you is hard. But I want to know what you're like under all that. Tell me about you."

I take a slow sip of the robust wine, trying to figure out how to start the conversation. He looks eager for answers. I can't decide if he really wants to know or if he's simply making small talk to get through dinner and onto the main course.

Us.

The wine warms me as I ponder how much to reveal.

"What do you want to know?"

"What do you do for a living?" he asks, scooping a heaping spoonful of sautéed mushrooms onto our plate.

"I'm in banking."

The thought of talking about that and the stupid project dumped in my lap instantly sours my mood. Not wanting to go there, I keep my reply curt, hoping he gets the hint as I drag my fork through the pile of mushrooms.

"Oh?" Paolo gives me a dubious look. "What kind of banking?"

"Investment banking," I say before shoving the fork in my mouth to avoid talking about work and moaning at the savory goodness of the food. His gaze darkens when he hears me.

"I want to be the reason you moan like that again."

Heat rises into my cheeks as he takes the fork from my hand and sets it on the plate. His hand returns to my knee, his fingers swirling the inside of my leg. When I meet his gaze, I notice the subtle flecks of gold in his brown eyes.

He wants me. He says it openly. Bold and unabashed. I'm done playing games. I'm done denying myself.

The last thing I want to do is talk about myself when his fingers feel so good. Light strokes against the inside of my thigh, and the pleasure of his touch nearly makes me lose my breath. I want this, I want him, and I want him now.

I push his hand away and grab his shirt, pulling him closer and kissing him hard and deep, pushing my tongue into his mouth, exploring and tasting. I can feel every muscle in my body tensing as we continue kissing, sucking, and nipping at each other. My hunger for him grows, pulsing into my pussy that aches to be filled by that hard cock straining against his dress pants.

His hand slides into my hair, my bun coming undone as he holds my head and takes control of the kiss. His touch is demanding and forceful, and he wants me to yield to his mouth. It's hot and unexpected. The innocent-looking kid in the bakery is getting downright obscene and raunchy with me in this corner booth, and I love it.

He swallows my moans and molds me to him. My hip lifts off the bench and my breasts press against his muscular chest. I'd climb onto his lap if we were anywhere else but here. His palm slides up my thigh until he reaches my ass which he kneads in quiet desperation. That's only temporary when he feels the edge of my thong and travels the fabric line between my legs. His fingertip slides toward my core, and he groans when he feels the wetness seeping from me.

I do not know why I've been holding back. I wanted him the second his package nearly sat on the tabletop. He's not only making me feel good, but he's also making me feel alive. He's awakening a passion and longing I haven't felt in a very long time. It's a delicious ache I want to indulge in.

"Fuck yeah," he mutters against my lips, the sound filling my mouth. It excites me that he's so turned on by me. That he considers me sexy and totally fuckable. It's a hell of a compliment that makes me understand why these old guys go for younger women. It's both an adrenaline rush of being a societal taboo and a complete ego boost.

"I'd take you right here if I could."

That finger swipes my clit. I jolt away, the bud so hard and sensitive that it wants to be smashed into oblivion by him. How many times could he go in one night? My ex was one and done. But he might be several, and now I'm the one saying *'fuck yeah'* in my head.

"I want that too."

"Let's get out of here," he continues in a hushed tone, his lips fluttering on my skin as he speaks. I shake his hand out of my hair.

"We just got here. I've barely touched my wine."

His finger is forced away from my pussy as I lean back, almost trapping his hand underneath me.

"I don't care about such things."

He reaches for his wallet and throws two hundred-dollar bills on the table to make his point. He flags down the maître-d, who immediately nods from across the restaurant. I'm embarrassed to think he could've been watching us, but it's my fault for getting carried away with this handsome stud.

"Paolo." I place my hand on his arm. The fabric from his coat is silky smooth under my touch. "I'm serious. I'd like to finish."

He takes my hand and kisses every knuckle before intertwining our fingers and placing it in my lap.

"So would I."

The candlelight dances in his brown eyes, entrancing me to where I agree with him. My desire for him crackles in the air between us. Our chemistry is rare. I've been with enough men to know that, and I don't want to waste it debating over finishing the wine and hors d'oeuvres.

"Sir?"

Paolo responds in Italian, the maître-d's eyes connecting with mine while they converse back and forth. He nods, collects our plate and the remaining food, and walks away.

"What did you say?" I ask after another man comes over to retrieve the wine bottle and glasses.

"They are going to wrap everything up so we can take it with us." He leans toward me, his lips at my ear once again. "Now you need to decide, your place or mine?"

His breath warms my skin, causing my shoulder to rise as his trimmed beard tickles my neck. My body sings with pleasure under the light touches against my skin. It's sensual and sexy, driving me crazy with want.

"I don't know."

I know it's a decision I could've made when I walked in here, but I hadn't thought that far ahead. I haven't been this horny in a long time, and it's blocking all rational thought. He could take me in his car or mine if he wanted to. The parking lot is dark enough that no one would see.

"I'd love to have you in my bed." His voice thickens, and his accent hits hard on the word bed. "I'll drive, and then we can retrieve your car in the morning."

Like a bolt of reality, I panic at the thought of spending the night with him, preferring to go home after we're done with this frivolous fling.

"No, I'll follow you," I say, moving away from him to see his expression.

A slow smile spreads long enough to kiss me quickly before the maître-d returns with a corked bottle of wine and our leftovers neatly tucked away in a bag that he hands to Paolo when he stands.

Paolo converses a few more times with the man and then offers me his hand to help me out of the booth. I thank the gentleman as well, and he bows deeply to me. I get the feeling that Paolo has been here before with the familiarity of their exchange, but I disregard it when he interlaces our fingers and leads me through the restaurant to the front door.

"Are you sure I cannot drive you?" he asks, holding open the door, and the crisp night air chills my skin. I shiver, clutching the edges of my dress, when his arm wraps around my shoulders and tucks me against him.

"I promise your car will be safe here, and I'll drive you back tonight then. As late as you want."

"No, I'll follow you."

5

TAYLOR

His home is charming. It's a one-story bungalow with a white-picked fence skirting the front yard and a swing on the wrap around porch. A small Italian flag drapes from one column and blooming roses cluster around the wide staircase leading to the front door. It looks more like an old grandmother's house than that of a hot, young stud.

He turns to me with a smirk.

"Welcome to my humble abode."

"It's so homey and not at all what I expected."

He's more of a mystery than I initially thought, and I am finding myself constantly surprised at the layers of him.

"It's my parents' old home. Come. You will see."

My eyes roam the porch as he fiddles with the keys in the lock and ushers me inside. The house is decorated with a mix of modern furniture and antique furnishings. Artwork clutters the walls, and family pictures are hung on the length of the mantle. He's from a large, seemingly close-knit family with smiling and similar faces greeting me, one I sort of recognize but cannot place. It's cozy with sophisticated tastes, letting me know he comes from money.

"Make yourself at home while I handle these," he says, breezing past me and tossing his keys onto a long entry table. He clicks on a few more lights down a hallway leading to what I assume is the kitchen. I take my time to look around the living room, absorbing the extensive collection of artworks—classic oil paintings contrasting against modern sculptures atop the end and coffee tables.

"You have exquisite taste," I say louder than intended when his hands sneak around my waist, his chest pressing into my back.

"I know."

His face nuzzles into my hair until his lips reach my skin, and I tilt my head to give him greater access. He takes full advantage by trailing kisses along the sensitive curve of my neck. His touch sends shivers down my spine, and a soft sigh escapes my lips as I melt into his embrace. The warmth of his body against mine and the tender affection in his actions create an intoxicating atmosphere.

I turn in his arms, facing him, and our eyes lock with shared desire. His lips capture mine until his tongue pushes into my mouth. He tastes like wine. It's intoxicating when he cups my neck with one hand, his thumb brushing my jaw to deepen the angle.

His kiss becomes more urgent as his hands travel upwards until they cup my breasts over the silky fabric of my dress. My nipples ache when he plucks them, sending currents of pleasure through my body. I lean into him and grasp his biceps, my nails digging into his sports coat, making me want to rip it from his body.

He breaks away from our kiss, his eyes smoldering with lust.

"I want you, mia cara."

"As do I."

His hand slips under the hem of my top, gently sliding it over my head before latching back onto my mouth. The coolness of the air sends shivers over my skin. I shudder when his lips trail down my neck to the hollow between my breasts. He wastes no time unclasping my bra with one hand while his thumb strokes a maddening circle around my hardening nipple.

When they fall free, he flashes me a content grin before taking my breast in his mouth and twirling his tongue over the erect peak. I moan, my head falling back to shove more of me into him. He repeats the process on the other breast, his soft hair tickling my delicate skin.

"More Paolo."

I exhale, tugging at his coat to move this along. I'm burning. My body is on fire, wanting so much more than he's giving. He is taking his time, drinking me in and cherishing every bit of my breasts and the space in between when I want him to take me fast and hard.

"I need you to fuck me. Now."

"Not here. Come," he murmurs against my skin, removing his coat and tossing it on the couch before leading me down the hallway, past the beautifully restored kitchen to a large bedroom at the back of the house.

He moves into the room, illuminated by a bedside lamp, the soft hue giving way to the comfort and elegance of his inner sanctuary. It's another room that blends vintage art pieces with modern furniture, resulting in an effortlessly chic vibe. And there it stands, a massive four-poster king-size bed, proudly taking center stage, beckoning our performance.

He stalks toward me, his lips glistening from sucking on my breasts. When his lower lip tucks into his teeth, I'm a goner.

"Strip."

He stops just out of reach and twirls a finger for me to

comply. It's hot as fuck, and even though his one-word command turns me the hell on, I need him to know he's not in charge. We're equals.

"You first."

He smiles, accepting my challenge, but takes his time unbuttoning his shirt. His thin fingers hesitate over the tie until he undoes it and tosses it on the armchair beside the bed. It's all slow and deliberate, building the anticipation before us. I squirm, wanting to be fucked hard and fast, then we can linger on each other.

He tosses his shirt on the floor, displaying a narrow waist and an athletic chest defined by some sport or physical activity. But my eyes settle on the dark brown hairline from his flat stomach into his dress pants.

"Your turn," he murmurs, extending a hand to me and drawing me closer to the bed. My heels clatter against his hardwood floor as I step toward him. The height difference is accentuated when I kick them off, making him even more desirable as he towers over me.

"That doesn't count. Take off the skirt."

I don't think shoes counted anyway, but I love how he's looking at me. Gone are all my inhibitions about age or stretch marks. He wants me as much as I want him by the pools of lust in his eyes, the shallow breathing of his chest, and the prominent bulge in his pants.

I turn my back, wiggling my ass for him to help me with the zipper on the back of my skirt, even though I could easily do it myself. He doesn't hesitate, sweeping it off my hips and down my legs so fast that I'm caught off guard when I'm suddenly bent over the side of the bed.

"You still want to be fucked?"

He's pressed against me. His belt digs into my tender skin and his fingers caress the waistband of my thong.

"Desperately."

With him trapping me against the bed, I rub my ass against his erection and glance over my shoulder. He's somehow got an unopened condom dangling from his teeth. With a wink, he quickly undoes his belt and pants, rips it open, and rolls it on. His thumb loops into my thong, moving it to the side when he grabs my hips from the bed to push into me. He's long and thick, filling me and then stopping.

"Fuck, I'm going to come," he groans, his accented words deep and sexy. "Wait."

I know exactly how he feels. If I could get a little thrust, I'd orgasm all over his cock almost immediately. My hands grip the bedding as my hips roll back to force some motion. He mutters something in Italian and then moves in and out so swiftly that the bed creaks.

The buckle of his belt slaps against my skin, the cold harshness an odd surprise against the plunging hardness of his cock. His hands splay across my hips. His thumb still loops into my thong and the fabric cuts into my flesh as he speeds up. It's a mix of pleasure and slight discomfort, all combining to be a mind fuck of a fucking. Something I didn't know I needed and something I desperately want as my burgeoning orgasm races toward an explosion.

Moans pour out of me as he's fucking me so good it's insane. It's fast, reckless and sloppy. The speed is beyond anything I've ever had, and I can barely hold on to the comforter. My hands slide across the luxurious thread count, and my knees buckle into the side of the bed. There's no fucking him back. He's too intense, too driven to give me exactly what I want. Fucked fast and hard with my breasts shoved into the mattress.

He's panting, sweating, and dripping onto my back. A sheen collects over my skin as my pussy clenches tightly around his long cock, hammering so deep I feel him bottoming out at my cervix. It's delicious and overwhelming, a push and pull contrast that I love as my orgasm tears through me with a scream of his name. It's euphoric and extending, lasting forever as I collapse on the bed, my cheek smashed to the comforter as he plows into me from behind.

Everything tightens, his hands on my hips, his body shoving into mine until a deep sated groan escapes his throat. It's hot and steamy, the smell of our mixed orgasms clinging in the air. I lay there enjoying him giving me precisely what I asked for.

"That was so good," he rasps, his thumb releasing from my thong as he slips out of my pussy that's still spasming in the wake of my climax. His hand cups my elbow, trying to help me to my feet, but my legs are too shaky, and I grasp the bedpost for help.

"Get in bed. I need a moment."

He gives me a quick kiss. I glance down at his cock as he's holding the ring of the condom in place, trying not to spill the contents. It's fuller than I thought, and I smile as he disappears into a white marble bathroom. Naturally, I want my partner to have as good of a time as I do, if not better, so seeing the evidence inflates my sex ego.

I forgo the bed, opting to trail after him into his designer bathroom. The allure of the space beckons and I step into a realm of luxury. The smooth marble stretches across the floor and halfway up the wall while intricate veins weave through the stone, adding depth and opulence.

A restored clawfoot tub stands in the center of the room with double vanities on each side. The spacious shower area boasts a frameless glass enclosure, offering a clear view of the same marble that lines the walls. The showerhead is positioned overhead with a smattering of hair and bath products in the niche in the wall. He finishes in the toilet, coming out with his pants at his ankles and smiling at me before moving into the closet.

"Your place is so nice," I say, my fingertips sliding over the smooth stone countertops to his collection of cologne bottles hugging the wall.

"You're surprised, yes?"

He walks out. His uncut cock points directly at me while I take in muscular thighs and defined calves. Yeah, he definitely goes to the gym every day to look like he does.

"Yes."

Our gaze meets in the mirror, his arms wrapping around me while his chest presses into my back. His dark eyes are not the smolder they were, more the playful expression in the bakery, and I like the variety. He walks me away from the counter, his hands moving up to cup my breasts again and caresses my nipples while he watches me.

"Tell me why?"

"Your age. I assumed it would be like a frat house with messes everywhere and a mattress on the floor."

I lean into him, my head resting against his collarbone as his hand skims over my skin to play with my clit. A sigh escapes my throat, and he partially smiles when he feels how wet I am.

"And you'd come to a place like that?"

That is a fair question. It makes me sound desperate, and I'm not. I straighten, feeling a touch offended at his question but more perturbed by the fact that I even considered visiting a house like that in the first place. When I begin to step away, his grip tightens.

"Forget I said that. Bend over."

His hand on my shoulder blade urges me forward. I'm still unsure why I'm not collecting my clothes and walking out. Other than the fact that I'm upset with myself while he's already moving on.

I slowly ease onto my elbows, asking, "Why? You want to watch your dick fuck me again?"

It's slightly immature, but his words still sting a bit.

"No, I want to watch your face when I fuck you. I want to see you come undone."

Him wanting to watch my expression is hot as fuck and something I've never heard before. The smolder is back, along with the heavy accented words, and just like that, I'm over being offended.

"You're already hard?"

He opens the drawer next to me, and a mix of his hair products and condoms cluster in the space before his hard cock pokes me in my cheek.

"You tell me."

The benefits of youth. A rapid recovery that I could get addicted to. He tears it open with his teeth, spitting the wrapper out to fall on the floor while pulling on my hips again.

"Arch your back and push out."

His voice is low and husky as his eyes dart from mine to his dick, then back. The countertop is cold against my breasts, a pleasant feeling against my heated skin as he slowly pushes into me. Gone is the furious pace to get off. This is savoring every inch of me as I slowly exhale.

"Again."

My command is breathless, eliciting a pleased smile from him. I close my eyes, my hand on the mirror, bracing myself while savoring how great his cock feels. His hand tickles my spine, rubbing up and down until it latches onto my shoulder to hold me in place. The pace is slow and deliberate, opposite to the pounding on the bed, and I love the difference.

Something clicks by my ear, and when I open my eyes, he's turned off the bright overhead recessed cans to a soft light illuminating the mirror. The faint hue casts almost a romantic candlelight effect in the room, intensifying the erotic feel of this experience.

"Look at me."

His hand moves past my shoulder to cup my throat, forcing

my back to arch more and expose the tops of my breasts. I adjust my hands to curve my body toward him, the shift in angle causing me to gasp as I stare into his dark eyes.

"Just like that."

Pinned against the counter by his deep cock, his hand holding my throat, and his fingers digging into my hip bone is an intensity I didn't know I needed. Relinquishing control, being fucked how he wants, and simply being allowed to feel everything he's doing to me is turning into the best sex of my life.

I don't have to concentrate on my mental game, focusing on an orgasm that may or may not come. His smooth, consistent strokes are building it in me. Changing angles ensures he hits the right spot and studies my face for confirmation. If he loves art, he's obviously studied the art of sex with how accomplished he is.

His stance widens, dropping his dick to the bottom of my pussy and sending the tip to the top. It's incredible, and I moan my pleasure.

"Your pussy is so wet. It's dripping out," he rasps, sounding proud with a slight smirk when our eyes meet. His hand slides up my throat, past my chin, turning my jaw to lean into me, and plants a kiss on my cheek.

"This is how I envisioned you at the bakery."

"Really?"

I can't say I wasn't thinking about fucking him but not in great details of positions and soft lighting. I push against my hands, attempting to straighten my back, when his hand leaves my face to cup the back of my thigh.

"Yes, you were so sexy in that little suit. I knew I had to see you like this. Had to have you screaming my name when you come."

Damn.

I did scream his name when I came. Hell, I'll do it again if he keeps this up.

"Put your leg up. Like this."

His hand is already gripping my leg to help me balance on one foot while my knee rests on the countertop.

"Oh shit," I murmur, the position amazing as it opens me up and allows his dick greater access to hammer my favorite spot.

"You look beautiful, mia cara."

His hand caresses my leg, leaving chills in its wake as his dick slows, stopping for a few seconds while he clenches his jaw. He's the beautiful one, having to stave off his orgasm more than once, which feeds my ego. I wiggle my ass, greedily wanting him to fuck me when the hand on my hip moves to my shoulder.

"More, Paolo."

He bites his bottom lip in concentration and then withdraws almost entirely, only to push slowly back in. We both moan, and I adjust my hands for better balance as he does it repeatedly. Going torturously slow until I'm back to begging him to fuck me like he just did.

"Fuck me," I plea, using the little leverage I have to quicken the pace.

"You're an impatient one. We'll have to work on that," he murmurs while keeping the same excruciating slow pace.

The fact that he said we'll have to work on that means this is not a one-night stand for him. And I don't know how I feel about it. I didn't expect to hear from him after tonight. I figured once I got in my car, that would be it. Hearing he has other plans in mind confuses me about my initial desire to keep it super casual.

I open my mouth to ask about it when he suddenly picks up the pace, giving me exactly what I want and taking my breath away when doing it. My hands squeak against the polished stone as I try to hold on to something. My thighs clench and my kneecap snuggles into the cabinetry groove.

He's fucking me fast and hard, his grunts filling the air between us at how hard he's working. My pussy is getting hammered in the best possible way. The euphoric feeling spreads out from my core throughout my body and sends a shiver over my skin as mini orgasms come one after the other. Precursors to the big one just out of reach until he yanks my leg off the counter, shoves my thighs together, and grips them so tightly it elongates my pussy.

It rockets the biggest orgasm out of me as I scream his name, echoing across the ceiling while my eyes close and my head falls forward. He continues pumping, muttering something I can't make out until he comes with a shout and rides his and mine all the way through. I collapse onto the counter, my body liquified from the series of orgasms leading to my final climax.

"Mia cara."

His hands roam my body, sending electric shocks through me with each touch, and I can barely move as he slips from my pussy. The emptiness is a void that I quickly want to be filled if he's going to keep making me feel this way.

"We should clean up."

"I don't think I can move."

I lie across his counter, my legs tingling and my body vibrating as he chuckles. The playful spark is back in his eyes when he kisses my shoulder and walks away to turn on the shower before ridding himself of the condom.

"I'll take that as a compliment."

Compliment, award, Noble Peace Prize, any will do.

6

PAOLO

I finish in the water closet and return to watch her as I wash my hands. She rises on her toes, flexing her legs which tightens her ass and makes it look amazing. Her worrying about the marks on her body is unbelievable. She's sexy as hell. Her head falling back in ecstasy, and the partial smile on her full lips sent me over the edge, chasing my release right after hers. What I wouldn't give to rid the barrier between us and feel her warm, slick walls on my cock directly.

The mere thought has me hardening for another round. I turn away to open the shower door, needing a moment before I invite her to join me. When I'm sufficiently in control again, I catch her checking me out—like she did in the cafe. I'd easily take her in the shower, press her against the glass wall and have my way with her.

"Will you join me?" My voice is raspy and deep, signaling my struggle.

"I think I should go."

Her foot stacks on top of the other in a flash of unexpected vulnerability. I tilt my head, questioning the sudden change in demeanor from sexy vixen to unsure woman.

"I don't want to get my hair wet."

It's a terrible excuse. One that has me immediately frowning as I shut the door and close the distance to her. It's been a fun night. One I want to continue into tomorrow morning. I like her more than I should for it only being one day.

Doesn't she see I'd like to spend more time with her? That's not something I usually do. Or at least not since the break-up. Most women I have tried to date my age annoy me with their superfluous chatter and general clinginess. Taylor's independence and somewhat aloof demeanor intrigues me. She hasn't once reached for her phone to snap a picture of our food to put on social media, obsess over make-up, or grill me about her outfit. It's refreshing and something I could get used to.

"What are you doing?" The hesitancy in her voice matches her body language.

"You'll see."

I throw open my drawer and toss a handful of headbands and hair ties on the counter to eliminate her excuse for running out of here. Especially as I want her to stay the night, to hold her in my arms and wake her up with my cock sliding in her pussy. Her arms close over her breasts, hiding them from view, which I instantly don't like, while her eyes glint hard.

"Ah, then you *do* have a girlfriend. I asked, and you said—"

"For tennis," I interrupt when she steps toward the bedroom to leave. I swiftly grab a hair tie, tilt my head back, and collect my hair to fashion it into a short ponytail. It gets her to stop. She eyes me cautiously as I take the headband I wore today and secure it over the front of my hair.

"And soccer."

Skepticism clouds her expression. While she doesn't move from her stance in the doorway, I grab one of each and descend on her.

"May I?"

Those dark green eyes bore into mine as she tilts her head

back. I reward her with a smile. She's so pliable once she's sure of my intentions, and I plan on being honest with her about everything. It's apparent someone hurt her long before me, and I won't contribute to that. Simple acts of trust and patience will benefit us both.

My hand dusts her skin as I collect her thick, long waves. I plant a kiss on the top of each bare shoulder. Her chin angles toward my face, wanting a kiss on the lips, but I deny her. Teasing is half the fun. When I move my face away from hers to concentrate on the task, a disappointed sigh loosens from her, and I stifle my smile.

"Taylor," I murmur when her hair is adequately out of her face and off her back before placing the headband to match mine.

When finished, I put one finger under her chin to raise it and press my lips to hers. She is sweet and moans when my tongue touches her. I'm a feign for everything oral, and I hope she is too. I have yet to eat her out and make her ride my face—all things we can do tonight once she agrees to stay. Her finger-tips press against my chest, a light pushing away to end the kiss, and now I am groaning.

"We're twins, Paolo."

We're nothing alike, but this sudden playfulness is opposite her usual serious demeanor, and it's very much welcome. I kiss the top of her head, right over the headband, before inter-locking our fingers and leading her to the shower. Steam pours out as I open the door, blurring her until I fan it away.

"After you, mia cara?" I say, in keeping with the lighthearted mood she started.

She skirts the steaming hot water, and I adjust it once inside. Her eyes roam over the body and hair products lining the shelf. I pick up the body wash, squeeze a generous amount into the loofah, and hand it to her. My favorite scent rises in the humid air, and I'm pretty pleased she'll smell like me tonight.

Her curves are luscious and tempting, begging for my mouth on those soft breasts that jiggle with each move. Her nipples are dark and erect, the areola wrinkled with hardness, and my mouth waters.

"Why are you watching me?"

"Why wouldn't I?" I remove the loofah from her hands and apply it to those sensational breasts. The ones I want to bury my face in as she rides me. "They're terribly dirty."

She gives me a knowing smile as I swirl the loofah around each breast. The suds glide down her stomach and disappear over her waxed mound. Those smooth lips are what I want in my mouth next. I shake away the idea of kneeling right here in the shower to taste them.

"I know something even dirtier."

She scoops the suds from her body and goes straight to my cock, which remains rock hard. My hand falters, then falls away, dropping the loofah on the tile floor as she strokes me in one hand and cups my balls in another. Her fist is light and lazy. Her eyes study my face as the showerhead sprays my back, shielding her from the water.

"That feels good. But I want back in there."

I cup her pussy, separating the lips and trying to ease two fingers inside when she steps back. Her hand falls away from my erection, and I stick my bottom lip out to display my displeasure.

"I've got to go, remember," she reminds me when I pick up on a hint of reluctance.

"I remember. But stay here with me. You can leave in the morning."

I'm negotiating again, something I find I'm doing more than I like. First the phone and now this. Any other woman would jump at the chance to spend the night, but I'm finding Taylor is more reluctant and stubborn than most. Something that both interests and frustrates me.

She retrieves the loofah from where it fell and squirts more soap on it, ignoring what I said. Disappointed, I turn into the stream to splash water on my face and scrub my beard before stepping aside for her turn.

Her naked body is even more beautiful when wet. The water makes her skin shimmer as it trickles down her flesh, sliding over the peaks and valleys and washing away the soap. I watch the water pool on her stomach, run down her hips and across her ass. I can't resist touching her.

That supple curve of her thighs when she separates them to wash has me stepping forward. My hands slide down her back to cup her ass and pull her against me. She arches her back, forcing her breasts into my chest, and my cock pushes into her pelvis bone, desperate to be inside her.

"Your skin is so smooth, I can't help myself," I admit, giving her a guilty smile when her hands rest around my neck. I take advantage of it by sweeping my hands down her back and ass, squeezing her cheeks.

"I try to take care of myself," she murmurs, rolling on her toes to give me a few innocent kisses before she steps away. I can tell she takes care of herself. Her flexibility was evident when I raised her leg and spread her out. Damn, that was hot watching my cock fuck her and seeing the expressions on her face while being fucked. A double gift.

"It shows."

Her efforts to finish cleaning are quick and efficient, all business-like. I don't like it. It makes tonight feel transactional and shallow. When she glances over her shoulder at me, I know she's ready to get out, so I promptly switch off the water and step out to get us towels.

"Thank you for tonight," she says as she takes the towel from my hand to secure around her curvy frame. The same curve I gripped hard as I fucked her hard from behind, testing how much she could take while bent over my mattress.

I try one last time by giving her a dazzling smile and saying, "You know, it doesn't have to end. It's late, and I wouldn't want you to fall asleep at the wheel on your way home."

"That's sweet, Paolo. But I doubt you'd let me sleep at all."

I offer her a sheepish smile, well aware that she has an inkling of the plans I have in mind. Abandoning the expectation that she'll acquiesce, I wrap the towel around my hips, allowing the rest of my body to breathe and dry naturally.

"Besides, I have to finish my presentation tomorrow."

She looks slightly worried. Our meeting at the café and dinner tonight probably ruined her plans. It was so worth it. I merely nod my understanding.

"Of course, I don't want to mess up your work."

She pauses at the mirror, our eyes meeting as I step close behind her. My chest dusts her back as she removes the headband and tie, letting her hair fall in luscious waves around her shoulders. I follow suit, tossing both of mine on the counter next to hers. It was fun while it lasted.

She looks beautiful. Her neck and chest flush from the hot water and her cheeks flush from sex. My palms caress down the sides of her arms, staring into those dark green eyes that stare back at me. What I wouldn't give to know what she's thinking. She smiles softly before pushing into my chest, and I step back, providing clearance as she walks into the bedroom to gather her things.

An awkward silence starts between us. Her brows pinch together in thought as she plucks her clothes from the floor and slips them on. If I knew her better, I'd inquire what's got her looking this way. If it's only about finishing her presentation, I'd offer to help. I've got nothing going on tomorrow and would gladly spend my Sunday with her.

I follow her lead in gathering my clothes from the closet and dress in close proximity to her to steal glances until she sets the towel on the bed to face me.

"What?" she asks, breaking the silence as we lock eyes again. The single word slips out. The curious intensity behind it casts me a lingering look as if she's possibly changing her mind about staying.

"Just admiring the view," I reply, to which she chuckles, a blush rising into her cheeks. Her eyes shift to the bed, which we could easily fall into, and she could ride my face or cock. Her choice this time. I smirk and raise an eyebrow as an invitation.

"Well, I hope the view lives up to your expectations," she retorts, matching my blatant hint with a bit of sass herself.

"Oh, it absolutely does."

I wink, my fingers toying with the bottom button of my shirt for a few seconds to see if she will change her mind. When she smiles and turns to leave the room to retrieve her blouse from the living room, I know all hope is gone. I finish dressing, slip on my shoes, and follow her.

By the time I get to the living room, she is dressed and waiting beside the door. Another sign that she's escaping. I'm struggling to grasp why she won't stay when it's evident she wants to. She's undeniably stubborn. I'll give her that.

I open the front door for her, strolling behind her to the car parked on the street beneath a lamp clouded with low hanging fog. My brain is firing on all cylinders, trying to come up with something to say as we round the hood and she unlocks her door.

Turning to her with a gentle smile, I murmur, "Text me once you're home so that I know you've arrived safely."

She nods and offers a warm smile in return, her hand reaching for the car handle.

"I will."

I give her a lingering kiss before she slips behind the wheel and starts the engine. With one final wave, which she reciprocates with a brief nod, she slowly pulls away from the curb.

As her taillights disappear into the misty night, I can't help but marvel at how unexpectedly fascinated I am by her. Our initial interaction was brief today, the texting more flirtatious, and then dinner leading to my place. I wouldn't have thought it would have happened this way, and I'm pleasantly surprised.

With a contented sigh, I turn and head back into my house. The uncertainty of where I stand with her hangs like the fog outside, thick and enigmatic. I'd love to see her again, to do all the things I long to do to her. Yet, a part of me also wants to get to know her beyond the sex. Her guarded nature is a mystery I'd love to solve.

That's it.

I'm seeing her tomorrow and won't take no for an answer this time.

7

TAYLOR

I wake up in the late morning, cocooned in the soft warmth of my sheets. It's the best sleep I've had in months. My body and mind are equally satisfied and refreshed. The morning light filters through the curtains, casting a gentle glow across the room. As I lazily stretch, a contented sigh escapes me.

My phone rests on the nightstand, and as I reach for it, I notice a couple of text messages. They're from Paolo, thanking me for texting him that I got home safely and wishing me a good morning. It's considerate and makes me smile.

I drop my phone on the bed beside me and let my mind wander back to last night. The memories rush in, a vivid replay of the steamy and spontaneous encounter. Our chemistry is magnetic, drawing us together. Every look, touch, thrust, and whispered word ignites a fire within that has me craving more.

The thrill of letting go and abandoning all concerns for a night of passion floods my core with wetness. He didn't care about my stretch marks or cellulite, not the way he fucked me twice from behind or the way his eyes glimmered in the ambient light in the bathroom mirror. No. His attraction to me was the same as mine for him, if not more.

It makes me hot thinking about it, and my hand drifts down my naked skin to circle my clit. It's not the same as sex, a far cry from it. I pretend my hand is his, twisting and plucking at my nipples while my fingers dampen. My eyes close as I think about his cock hammering the shit out of me. The way my legs strained and tensed, holding back a beast that was unrelenting in pounding me until my face was smashed into the mattress.

As my small orgasm builds, it's nothing compared to the powerful ones he forced out of me. Orgasms I didn't have to concentrate on and work for like I did with other men. Not with Paolo. Our shared attraction and intense chemistry made me horny and raring to go the second I walked into that restaurant. I was on the fence driving over there, telling myself that I could leave, go home, and work on the presentation. The moment I laid eyes on him, all dressed up for our date, I knew I deserved to partake in the deliciousness he was offering. I want that deliciousness now.

I swirl faster, trying to race my climax to the forefront, when my phone pings, interrupting memories of us. With a sigh and a fleeting orgasm, I pull myself from my thoughts and look at my phone. It's him again, wanting to know if I want to meet for brunch. Perhaps this can go beyond a simple one-night stand and proceed into a weekend fling—one more day of living in the cocoon of Paolo and me before I return to reality tomorrow.

The unfinished presentation nags at my conscious, equal in importance to going another round or two with him to officially obliterate my sexual dry spell. I wrestle with myself, knowing the responsible thing to do is to turn him down, grab a coffee from the kitchen, and open my laptop. Naturally, I do the irresponsible thing and text him back. He quickly responds, as if his phone was in his hand, waiting for my reply. That's a nice feeling.

Excellent! Come over in an hour.

I will have everything ready.

Wait a minute. I thought he meant food, which I am starving for after the night's non-existent dinner and missing breakfast this morning. My fingertips fly across the letters, about to quash this whole thing as I can't spend the day in bed with him. However, last night went very quickly.

Smooth, Paolo. I thought you meant food at a restaurant. Not us eating each other.

He sends a picture of him smiling shirtless in his kitchen, the counter covered in ingredients with a vintage stove behind him.

I like the way you think mia cara.

Sustenance first.

Each other second.

Once again, I debate. This is not what I thought when he invited me, but nothing Paulo does is what I expect. Even though it makes me a bit uncomfortable, I like his spontaneity. When I take too long to respond, he sends a follow-up message.

:/

What does that mean?

You take too long.

You won't come.

:/

I chuckle. He's perceptive, even when texting. As my fingers hover over the keyboard, I think about how much time my presentation needs to be complete and how much time I can spend with him.

I can only spend two hours there.

Why?

Because I have to work.

Not that I have to justify myself to him, but it's important that he knows my time constraints up front.

Why?

I have to finish the presentation I didn't get done yesterday. Some hot Italian interrupted me.

You think I'm hot?

He sends me another picture where he's donned a frilly feminine apron and has a dusting of flour across his forehead. His eyebrow is up and inquisitive while those deep brown eyes stare into the camera. It's cute, and I'm chuckling again.

You know you are.

Possibly.

But come.

Please.

To hell with it. Two hours in and out, then back home, finish work, and go to bed. I smile as I text him.

I'll be over in thirty minutes.

:)

He sends me a pin drop of his address as if I forgot where he lives. Then a demand that reminds me of last night.

Don't wear any panties.

He had no problem fucking me with them on last night, but I'll play along.

I won't ;)

I'm getting hard.

He sends another picture, his apron moved aside, and his tan sweatpants pulled down to showcase that gorgeous cock. I can see its full size with the sunlight pouring into his bright kitchen. I'm instantly tingling in my sore nether regions, and a thrill of excitement runs through me.

Gorgeous. I'm getting off, so I can be over there. Remember, two hours max.

:/

I receive a follow-up photo of him frowning, his cock still at full erection, and I ignore it. I lock my phone and swing my legs over the edge of the bed to get ready. The thought of being with him again, rolling around in his bed and sharing more intimate moments, fuels my eagerness to race through my morning routine with newfound motivation.

Dressed and ready, sans underwear, I take a deep breath and head out the door, my heart beating fast in anticipation as I drive to his place. His neighborhood has a church in the center, patrons pouring into the place about to be absolved of their sins while I commit new ones. The thought has me squirming when I pull into his long driveway and open my door to see him coming out of his with a ridiculous chef's hat added to his frilly apron.

His smile is quick and easy, and he jogs down the pathway to stand at my door. The second I have it open, he helps me out and gives me an indecent kiss.

"Hi."

His voice is welcoming with a hint of desire that has me looking down to see his erection has gone down. His hand squeezes mine, and he looks guilty when my gaze returns to his.

"I had to jerk off just now. You really get me going."

His arms envelop me, encircling my waist in a firm embrace. His hand instantly kneads my ass while his lips find their way to my neck. I lightly hold his waist, the frilly apron almost sheer to the touch, as his body wash swirls into my nose.

"I thought we were eating first."

He groans against my skin, a noisy protest that clearly communicates what he wants first. When he straightens, his chef's hat is askew, a lock of his hair falls forward, and his lower lip juts out.

"Compromise. I eat off you."

"Come on."

I roll my eyes and walk the path leading into his house while he trails behind, grumbling the entire time. I get a whiff of something delicious smelling and proceed to investigate. The aroma of freshly brewed coffee mingles in the air the closer I get to his kitchen. His bare feet quietly tread behind me as I see more progress has been made with the ingredients smattered all over the island in the picture.

"It looks like the bakery from yesterday."

A half dozen decadent croissants sit in the center, each one a masterpiece. They're dusted with powdered sugar, adorned with a glistening yellow topping, and crowned with a raspberry nestled in the center. Next to them, croissants are filled with ham and cheese, and the contents ooze temptingly from the middle. And, of course, shimmery and mouth-watering macarons complete the display.

"You made all this?" I ask in awe, turning to him as his eyes sweep over his handiwork before returning to meet mine.

"This is . . . not much. My mamma would think this is a lazy man's breakfast."

His accent is thick as his hands gesture wildly while he talks as if they need to explain it too—another endearing thing about him.

"Well, I usually have a cup of coffee. If this is a lazy man's breakfast, I don't know what your mom would call mine."

His laughter rings out, a rich sound that fills the air.

"She'd probably say coffee is a drink, not breakfast, and then tell you that you're too skinny," he quips, his eyes twinkling.

I raise an eyebrow playfully, feigning offense.

"Hey now, I'll have you know that I've been known to enjoy a good breakfast or two."

He steps closer, his gaze locking onto mine.

"Then let's enjoy this lazy man's breakfast together."

His proximity gets my heart racing, and our undeniable attraction sparks to life again. It's as if every interaction, every shared word, has me wanting to attack him.

Settle down, cougar. I mean, Taylor, this is only a weekend fling.

8

TAYLOR

Breakfast is both casual and exhilarating. It's been a long time since I've connected with someone as quickly as I do with Paolo. The conversation flows naturally over various topics, like his passion for photography and travel. These subjects are dear to him as he speaks about them with infectious enthusiasm.

His hands gesture wildly with every word that spills from that beautiful mouth, causing his chef hat to fall somewhere in the middle of his stories. He tells me about the hidden gems he's discovered in far-off places and the breathtaking moments he's captured through his camera lens. It's clear that he has a unique perspective, coming from Italy and being able to travel extensively through college before obtaining his master's degree.

He shares his plans to start a travel blog about his experiences and shows me his website under development. I don't doubt that his blog will be a remarkable journey of the world through his eyes.

Over breakfast, it becomes clear that our connection goes

beyond physical attraction. Genuine compatibility, shared interests and values make the time fly. Meeting someone who piques my curiosity and stirs a wanderlust in my soul to travel is unusual. The more time I spend with him, the more the years between us fade into nothingness.

"I insist on doing the dishes since you made all this." I lean away from the table, feeling fuller than I would've preferred, especially if we're having sex after this. "I ate too much."

He grins. A mischievous glint in his eyes as he replies, "Well, that's a tempting offer, but I know of a more enjoyable way to work off those calories than washing dishes."

I stand, feeling a delightful warmth spread through me at his playful response.

"You have a point. But I'm too full for that right now. Let's clean up and then go from there."

His bottom lip juts out as it did last night when I said I was leaving. It's endearing, but I ignore it when he stands. As we clear the breakfast dishes, our conversation remains light-hearted, filled with playful banter and flirtatious exchanges.

"By the way, you're not just good at making breakfast. You're also a fantastic kisser," I say when he leans in to hand me a plate.

"Flattery will get you everywhere."

He steps closer, his hand brushing against mine as he reaches for another plate.

"Is that so?"

"Yes, mia cara, but I suspect you already know that."

I playfully roll my eyes, enjoying the sexual innuendos between us. He quickly kisses me on the side of the head before grabbing the last dish. Once the dishes are done, I turn to him with a sly grin.

"Now, about that other work you mentioned . . ."

"I believe it's time for that, don't you?"

His eyes sparkle. The apron adorning his bare chest is whipped off in a flash. His hands reach for my hips, pulling me to him.

"How about we continue this conversation somewhere more comfortable?"

His voice is low and seductive, and my heart races with excitement.

"Lead the way," I respond, a knowing smile on my lips.

He releases my hips to interlock our fingers and leads me down the hallway to his bedroom. The room is bathed in bright sunlight streaming in from the three windows slated above his bed. Soft music plays in the background, adding to the casual ambiance of this lazy Sunday. The world outside and my work worries fade as I intend to lose myself in him again.

"Now, where were we?"

He towers over me, and it's the sexiest thing ever. He makes me feel small, and at my height, only tall guys can do that. It's primal and archaic thinking, something I usually hate in my male-dominated industry. Yet, in the bedroom, it's a huge turn on.

"Oh yes, strip."

"Excuse me?"

The deep octave of his voice is a straight shot to my pussy, no doubt about it. The directness of his command surprises me.

"You heard me, Taylor."

That roll of the 'r' in my name gets me every time. I quickly shed my clothes to stand naked before him. His eyes are smoldering and serious despite the smile on his lips.

"Happy now."

His hands are planted on his narrow hips, causing the waistband of his sweatpants to dip lower, revealing more of his happy trail.

"No. On your knees. I want to see those pretty pink lips wrapped around my cock."

Either it heated to a thousand degrees in here or it heated to a thousand degrees with how commanding he's being. I can't decide if I like or hate it, but I'm immediately turned on by it.

"Down."

His thumbs tuck into his waistband for them to fall to the floor. His veiny cock bounces out, erect and ready to receive the attention it deserves after last night's performance.

"I should be the one bossing you around. After all, I'm older," I sass, unsure if I should sink to my knees or wait for his next move. The smile falls from his face as seriousness takes over, and I tilt my head, wondering what it means.

Without a moment's pause, he swiftly lifts me, playfully tossing me onto the bed. The suddenness of it catches me off guard, and just as I'm about to speak, he pushes my knees toward my chest and licks from the bottom of my pussy to the top of my clit.

"Boss me around then. Tell me what you want," he murmurs against my skin as his dark eyes turn black with lust between my legs. "Is this what you need?"

Need. Want. Crave. Require. Any word will do.

His tongue swirls fast circles on my clit. It's incredible and sensitive. Intimate and passionate.

"Oh yes! Fuck yes, Paolo!"

I pant as I reach for a pillow to shove under my head to get a better view of what he's doing to me. His hair falls forward. The softness tickles my inner thigh, adding to the tantalizing sensations rising from my core. His hands press into the back of my thighs, forcing them wider apart and plunging his tongue deeper.

"You taste delicious."

He hums against my flesh, sucking a lip between his before

diving his tongue back into my pussy. I gasp and squirm, the intensity too much and not enough at the same time.

"More. I need more."

His shoulders press against my hamstrings, trying to get deeper and deeper until he's tongue fucking me. I gasp, loving how enthusiastically he's eating me out, alternating between sucking the soul from my clit and plunging his tongue in and out of my wet pussy.

"I need you to fuck me. I need you inside me."

His hand falls away from my thigh to find my mouth, plunging two fingers inside for me to suck with the same intensity he's sucking on my clit.

"Tell me, Taylor. Fingers or cock?" he taunts, blowing against my clit and sending shivers over my skin. He doesn't remove his fingers from my mouth. Instead, he pushes another one in. Fucking my mouth as I want him to fuck my pussy. It's hot and confusing at the same time.

He switches positions while my brain is still processing what is happening. The fingers I was sucking are now pushing inside me and filling me up in the best way possible while his cock taps my lips for entry.

"Both for you."

I lick my lips and collect enough saliva to welcome him in. His fingers are vigorous in finding my sensitive spot and fucking the shit out of me. His cock is slow and patient, allowing me to suck him off at my pace. The contrast makes my brain spin out of control, unable to concentrate on anything and everything at the same time. I cup his balls as he cups my head, keeping me where he wants me as his fingers plunge in and out.

The slow build of my orgasm rockets to the forefront. The pressure coming so deep from within, it's the most intense feeling I've ever had. My body tightens, and my hips rise to create a straight channel into my pussy for his vigorous fingers to hammer that spot.

I lock eyes with him, on the verge of free falling into my climax. He shifts his gaze to watch my pussy while mine close to blinding darkness. I come the hardest I ever have. The buildup and subsequent release of yellow swirls behind my eyelids has me collapsing in ecstasy. His cock slides from my lips as a pattern of shock waves courses over my body.

I open my eyes when he grunts, watching long strings of his cum paint my breasts and torso. He's pulling tightly on the crown of his cock as it spurts all over me. Something about seeing him handle his meat like that has me leaning up and welcoming it back into my mouth. I want to finish him off in the best way I can after he gave me one of the most intense climaxes of my life.

He rattles off something in Italian while his head tilts toward the ceiling and his eyes close. His mouth parts and his tense expression eases into pleasure. He's stunning. Being the only one who gets to see him this way stirs something in me. Gentle are his fingertips that caress my cheek as his hips stop pumping into my mouth when he opens his eyes to look down at me.

"That is the best, yes?"

He doesn't need to ask. He has only to look at me to know it's more than the best. My heart is beating a mile a minute. My body is completely immobile, and my legs are splayed as I bask in the rightness of us. His cock slides from my mouth once more as he moves to stand at the side of the bed.

"I can't move."

My breath comes out in pants while my heart continues to pound.

"You squirted. A lot."

That proud smile returns to his face. As if making me squirt is a badge of honor. It is because he's one of only a couple that has ever made me do it. And never with fingers. Maybe he deserves a merit badge. He sure did last night.

"That's why it was so intense." I curl up to see my wetness and his cum mixed all over my body. "I'm a mess."

I collapse back to the pillow. His cock is at eye level with me. It must be painful being erect all the time.

"Our beautiful mess."

His voice is husky and pleased when he extends a hand to help me. I can't feel my legs and I certainly don't want to move. It's a necessary evil to clean up. I inch to the edge of the bed and sit up for the fluids to slide down my body. He watches, bearing that same badge winning smile of his.

"I like how you look," he mutters, depositing a kiss on the crown of my head before walking into the bathroom.

I follow him, but as I glance at his bed, I gasp, and my hand covers my mouth. He steps out of the bathroom, concern etched on his face to see what's startled me.

"What's wrong, mia cara?"

I merely point at the massive wet spot I left on his bedding.

"Like I said, you squirted a lot." His fingertips skate down my arm to draw me close to him. "Now kiss me."

My hands move to his chest as I angle my lips to meet his in two hastily planted kisses. Yet, my eyes return to his bed, wondering how soaked it is.

"I can help you wash it. I mean, this comforter may have to go to the dry cleaners, and if we get it off now . . ."

I break away from his hold to tug at the corner of his bedding, knowing it's expensive and not something we can stuff into his washing machine.

"Look at me."

He stops my hands by clasping them within his and forcing me to face him.

"I like it. I did that to you. I made you squirt while my cock was down your throat. It couldn't be any better."

The vulgarity with which he describes it makes me flush with embarrassment. I look somewhere around his collarbone when his finger captures my chin and drags it up to look at him.

"I want to do it again and again. Let's drench my entire bed." He chuckles, then tightly wraps me into his arms for my cheek to lie against his defined chest. "Then we can do the same at your house."

The harsh truth of that statement tightens my chest, constricting my lungs. It's clear he doesn't want this to come to an end. It's not just a weekend fling for him. The more time we spend together, the more I want to be with him. He's intriguing, playful, gorgeous, and amazing in bed. But will we continue to go out, or will it just be casual sex? Reduced to a text emoji that I see on social media posts? I decide to test the waters.

"Would you go out with me?"

My words are muffled against his skin and hang in the air. He leans back, his chest expanding as he gently nudges me away from his body. His eyes lock onto mine as I wait for his response.

"Are you asking me out on a date?"

His hair falls forward, a strand sticking to his lip until he shakes it from his face. His answer is a breath away.

"I was sure hoping you would, as this weekend is coming to a close, and I want to see you again."

A warm feeling collects in my chest. I'm not just a booty call or some novelty for him to sample. He really wants to date me, and I like the idea more and more.

"Really?" I ask, my fingers gently stroking the warm skin of his ribcage.

"I do," he replies, his voice soft and sincere.

I can't help but feel a rush of happiness. It's clear that this connection is something more than I expected, and it fills me with a sense of excitement about what lies ahead. I haven't had this type of closeness in a very long time. I didn't know how much I missed it until now.

His lips dust mine before he pulls away and looks down at our bodies. The cum and fluids on me have transferred to him, and he throws back his head for a carefree laugh.

"We should shower," I suggest, my hands gently falling from his body. His hands mirror my movement, relinquishing their hold.

"I'll get the hair ties."

9

PAOLO

She's so damn sexy. My cock agrees, wanting back in her soft folds and trying to get inside her while in the shower. I get close until she pushes me away, complaining that condoms don't work in the water. I groan, respecting her wishes even though I'd easily make her moan and come without them.

"It's now my personal goal to make you squirt every time we have sex."

"You're ridiculous."

Her green eyes brighten when she laughs before shoving me under the cascading water to rinse the suds from my body. I close my eyes, tilt my head into the spray, and replay what just happened.

Her soft, warm pussy sucking in my fingers while her hot mouth sucked my cock sent me over the edge. And damn if she didn't look beautiful while doing it. Her body was on display, spread out for me to do whatever I wanted. I filled two holes— who wouldn't bust a nut in minutes?

The way her eyes squeezed close in concentration, her tongue working my tender foreskin, and her thighs pushing her pussy further into my hand, it was too fucking much. Something we'll repeat every time I see her. A must. A mandatory requirement from now on.

And her embarrassment over my bed. It's an enchanting surprise from the ordinarily independent woman. Then to ask me out, fidgeting in my hold as if she was nervously awaiting my answer, fucking icing on the cannoli. I can't believe how lucky I am to have picked that café at that time to discover this rare beauty.

"Are you going to continue hogging the water, or can I rinse off?" she asks, full of sass. When she hangs the cord to my loofah around my hard cock, leaving it dangling in the air, I laugh. She shrugs, her hands cupping the side of my body as we change positions.

"I thought it could be useful for something while we're in here."

She turns toward the spray, letting the water carry the soap down her soft body. I remove the loofah, squeeze out the excess, and place it on the hook. My hands come around to cup her full breasts, kneading them before twisting the nipples into stiff peaks.

"He could be more useful if you let him back in."

I stoop to plant kisses down her neck, burying my face in her skin and trying to bite it.

"No hickeys. I have a very important meeting in the morning," she scolds, edging away from my hold to turn off the faucet and escape out the door.

She plucks one of the towels from the ledge I retrieved for us and starts drying off. The steam on the shower walls blurs my view, and I dart out as she's wrapping it around her body. I pout, sticking my bottom lip out when I look at her.

"I'm serious. If you want to leave a hickey, it has to be under my clothes where no one can see it."

I jump at the opportunity, ready to give her one on each of my favorite breasts when she plants a hand on my forehead.

"I didn't mean now."

"Taylor." I groan in protest, straightening. "You can't offer and then take it away."

She looks at the beads of water still covering my body and points to the towel. I don't care if I'm dripping on the bath rug.

"I can and will. Plus, I want to pillow talk before I leave."

I groan again. No hickeys, and she must leave. She exits the bathroom, and I follow, watching her throw back the layers of bedding as she pats to find dryness.

"I'll lay in the wet spot. I don't care, but why must you leave so soon? We didn't even have sex yet?"

She whirls around on me, her eyebrows high as she points to the bed.

"What do you call that?"

"You know what I mean. I want inside you." I point to my hard cock. "He wants to be where these were." I wiggle the fingers that made her squirt, knowing if my cock could hammer the same spot, it would be a delicious waterfall again.

"I want to make you feel good again."

A contemplation look appears when she glances at the bedside clock.

"One hour, including pillow talk, at least twenty minutes of it."

I never said I had a problem with pillow talk. Where she got that idea is beyond me. I enjoy sharing things with her and watching her think and react to what I'm saying. It's part of why we are so good together.

"Five minutes of talking. Fifty-five minutes of fucking."

I'm constantly negotiating with her. I'm beginning to dislike it immensely.

"Fifteen minutes of talking. And forty-five minutes of sex," she counters while I tug at the corner of her towel knotted against her breasts.

"Ten minutes."

"Deal."

The towel falls to the floor when she crawls into bed, moving to the dry side and leaving me with a slight remnant of the wet spot. The cool sheets feel amazing against my damp skin. But the stunning woman lying in my bed, snuggling up to my side and laying her head on my chest, is the best feeling of all. Her thigh settles between my legs. The heat from her pussy against my hip has me drawing in a ragged breath. All I can think about is getting through the next ten minutes until I put her on top of me and make her ride me backward.

"What should we talk about?"

Her head angles up for those dark green eyes to look at me expectantly. Not that I don't want to talk. I'm just too busy counting down the time on the clock.

"Paolo, I'm serious."

Caught off guard, I tighten my arm around her, my fingers grabbing her ass cheek while concentrating on words and not her flesh.

"I talked about me and my interests all morning. Now, it's your turn. Tell me about this big presentation that's taking you away from me in fifty-nine minutes."

She frowns but obliges with a long sigh.

"Well, I work with this stupid idiot that thinks he's the smartest guy in the room, but he's an ass. Condescending, demeaning toward women, and generally a snake in the grass. He's always doing sneaky shit, and everything is for his benefit. Anyway, the Chairman asked me to help with his VIP client, who's upset about what this idiot is doing. I have to get to the bottom of the customer's complaints, see where he messed up, and then present my findings tomorrow."

"Sounds important," I murmur, releasing her cheek to trace

circles on her lower back as she places her hand on my chest to rest her chin. "But why you?"

"Why me? Because my work is impeccable. I don't take shortcuts. I don't cheat the system and do the right thing all the time. It angers me that we're equals, and he gets to keep his job despite all the shady shit he does. I've wondered if he has compromising photos of the Chairman because it's the only explanation for how he keeps his job."

"From what I've seen of you, you're incredibly capable and driven. They're lucky to have you helping this important client."

I understand her frustration. It's why I do what I do because I believe in right from wrong. Hearing she does too, makes me like her even more. A faint smile tugs at her lips, and she snuggles closer.

"Thank you, that means a lot. But it's a boys club up there. Very few females are in management, and only two are at my level. It's a dog-eat-dog type of climate. One mistake, and I'll lose my chances of being promoted."

I tuck her hair behind her ear and stroke her cheek.

"I have no doubt you have the intelligence to navigate that boys' club and come out on top. And when you do, it will be a victory not just for you but for all the women in your company who aspire to follow in your footsteps."

Her face breaks out into an immediate smile, so happy and radiant at what I said that I could start fucking the shit out of her right now if we didn't have seven more minutes of pillow talk remaining.

"If only those old farts at Williamson Cooper thought so," she huffs before kissing my chest and laying her head on it.

Williamson Cooper.

My pulse races beneath her temple, something she will discover as her head lies against the throbbing organ. Guilt washes over me as I realize who she is—Taylor Woods, Senior

Vice President of Client Relations at Williamson Cooper. The very person I'm to be meeting with after visiting with Ted. The pieces fall into place, and my gut tightens.

She's the person I was supposed to coordinate with before coming, but she was out of town in Pittsburgh, immersed in a steel acquisition deal for her client. The 'old farts' she's complaining about, the ones she's trying to navigate in that dog-eat-dog environment—they're the same people who know my father. The same ones who hired me. Nepotism at its finest. Taylor will hate that even more.

Fuck.

I swallow hard, suddenly feeling cold despite the heat between us. I can't help but wonder how this weekend will affect our working relationship and whether it will jeopardize the assignment I've been given. If this shady fellow is the one I'll be investigating, that puts me as her direct colleague and probably not allowed by the company policy.

It could jeopardize what Taylor and I have started. Connections like ours aren't easily made, and I've enjoyed every minute of my time with her. My job at Williamson Cooper, my future, and even this budding relationship—all seem to hang in the balance.

Cazzo.

And what about Taylor? Will she face backlash or scrutiny if they find out about us? Will they permanently shut her out of the 'boys' club' for doing what many older men do with younger women?

I glance down at her, my chest aching as I rub her hair and receive a soft moan of appreciation. Do I tell her now? Confess what I know? Or wait until tomorrow? In the back of my mind, I know what the right thing to do. But I am selfish and fear this will end here and now in the next two minutes of remaining pillow talk. Not that I can't forgo the sex. I can and will if necessary. What I can't let happen is for her to walk out that door and never have this again.

It's a lose-lose situation, but at this moment, I want to take my losses tomorrow and savor her today. I want to hold on to this connection, bask in her presence's warmth for just a little longer. The clock on the nightstand reminds me that time is running out. I can't help but wonder if this stolen moment of intimacy is worth the risk of losing her forever.

"Time's up, buttercup," she says, her voice playful and teasing as she shifts her face to look at me.

Her green eyes sparkle with the same playfulness. I close my eyes momentarily, knowing this is my last chance to make the right decision. To do the right thing by her.

I'm torn as I feel her warmth against my chest and the soft caress of her lips on my flesh. The truth lingers on the tip of my tongue, ready to be spoken, but I hesitate. I can't bear the thought of this moment ending, of her walking away from us right now.

In that fleeting moment, I make a choice—a selfish one. I lean in and capture her lips in a lingering kiss, a silent promise to myself that I'll address all this tomorrow when she finds out. Right now, I want to make love to her for the first and last time.

10

TAYLOR

Talking about work on the weekend has never been my idea of a good time. I've always heard it referred to as the 'Sunday Funday killer' on social media, and it couldn't be more accurate. Sundays are supposed to be a time to relax and recharge, not dwell on the stress of the workweek ahead and work on damn projects for lazy colleagues. It dampens my mood when talking about it.

I don't expect it to affect Paolo as deeply as it does. He turns quiet and introspective. I can't help but notice the shift in his mood. I understand my work may not be as fascinating as his travel exploits, but I anticipated him being a bit more talkative.

While he's supportive and says everything I want to hear about my work situation, there's an uneasiness in the air. It's a departure from his ordinarily jovial manner, and it leaves me wondering if I've inadvertently become the Sunday Funday killer.

My concerns about the shift in his mood vanish when he rolls me onto my back. All worries about work or other distractions melt away as he kisses me from head to toe, sucking and relishing various parts of my body. He even makes it a point to leave a hickey on each breast after asking permission first. It's harmless and cute. And who cares since we are the only two seeing them?

His mouth moves down my body to my clit and sucks my soul from me, one orgasm at a time. When I'm about to return the favor, he sheaths that delicious cock and leisurely pushes inside me. He eases in, opening me up so deliberately slow that I sigh with satisfaction.

My hands skim over his smooth skin to grab his tight ass, cupping the underside to push him in deeper when I open my legs wider. The dark brown of his eyes is an endless abyss as he stares into mine. His expression is concentrated and distant. I can't shake the feeling that something I said has bothered him, casting a shadow over our sex.

The fun and carefree atmosphere when we negotiated the pillow talk evaporated when he stiffened at the mention of my work. I can't understand why that would cause him concern, but it seems to have temporarily fractured our chemistry. I want to bridge that gap. To address whatever just happened.

"Are you okay?" I murmur, my hand moving to cup his cheek and stroke his beard with my thumb. It's a long few seconds before he dusts my lips once, twice, and then buries his face in my neck.

"You feel amazing."

The absence of an answer, of any reassurance or explanation, only deepens my concern and waves red flags in my mind. I can't help but wonder what's going on in his. What might be causing this sudden distance between us? Distance allows doubts to sneak in and ruins relationships. Distance causes marriages to fall apart and men to find younger, prettier women to be their mistresses.

My heart races with worry, and I'm left to grapple with the uncertainty of the situation, desperately hoping that he'll eventually open up and share whatever is troubling him.

He makes slow, sweet love to me—the opposite of the other times and far more intimate. Moans, groans, and grunts replace the previous laughter, banter, and chatter. Both giving what we want and taking what we need. There are no changing positions or watching his dick hammer my sensitive spot until I squirt all over him—none of that.

I'm buried underneath him. The hard planes of his body pin me to the mattress as I take his cock repeatedly, the buildup so slow that it's keeping my orgasm at bay.

"Please, Paolo," I beg, winding my legs around his waist and spurring him to fuck me harder. "I need more."

"Not yet." He shakes his head and says, "I want this to last."

The roll of his hips, the flex of his ass, and the throbbing of his massive erection inside my pussy, drives me mad with need. Never giving me the release I want and never letting me come to completion.

"I want to come. I want you to come," I repeat, gripping his shoulders to force him to move faster.

I need him to finish me off. To make my toes curl and my mind blank. I need him to pound me like he did yesterday, fast and hard. This lovemaking is good, but it's an appetizer when I need a steak dinner.

"Please, Paolo. Make me yours."

That does the trick. His thighs tuck under my hips as he speeds up. His eyes are glued to mine. His teeth catch his bottom lip, and his brows knit together when he pushes into me as deeply as possible. I grind my hips with him, wanting to feel his cock and the delicious friction of our thrusting as he fucks me harder.

He lets out a guttural sound that escapes through his teeth, and it's the hottest thing I've ever heard. His body stiffens, and I know he's close, so I lift my hips and place my feet flat on the bed, giving him room to slam into my pussy.

"Oh fuck, mia cara," he moans as the head of his cock hits me at my core.

"More," I whisper harshly, and his pace picks up again. I feel my stomach tightening and my pussy clenching. I'm seconds away from exploding around his cock.

"Come," he demands as his hand cradles my head. "Come now."

That's all it takes for me to burst. I come undone beneath him, muttering his name repeatedly. My toes curl against the mattress, and my pussy contracts around his cock, milking him of every drop as he comes with a low growl.

The sweat between our bodies seals us together. When he collapses on me, his face buries in my neck, and I feel the perspiration in the soft strands of his hair. Our panting is in unison. Our pulse is fast and in sync. Even though we are as close as two people can physically be, I feel miles apart emotionally.

I stare at the ceiling, wondering what to say. The intensity from lovemaking to fucking was terrific, but the sizzling chemistry was an echo, replaced by a mostly silent and somewhat haunted looking Paolo.

"Are we done?"

The question applies to both the sex and this weekend's fling. With the walls going up on his side and the cold shadow of his distant demeanor, I need clarification that I'm not the only one feeling this. I need him to confirm what I thought could go on for a bit longer is actually ending. Maybe we won't have that date after all. Something changed within him that makes me think this is the end.

"Is this over?" I repeat when he doesn't answer me.

He stirs, lifting fractional inches until our eyes meet. The seriousness in his expression, the slight frown on his lip, and the sincere tilt of his head make my chest ache. There is a sudden sadness in his look, and the longer he stares, the more worried I get about those damn red flags.

Did he use me? Or did I use him? Were we using each other to get over something or someone neither knows about? Was I foolish in thinking it could last longer? Foolish for asking him out and believing it would happen?

Doubts tumble over each other until I'm pushing against him, wanting to escape this awkwardness and forget I ever believed it possible for an older woman and a younger man to date.

"I certainly hope it's not over, Taylor," he finally says, ceasing my movements to cup my cheek. "I like you. I like this. I want to see where this goes."

His admission brings a glimmer of hope. I can't help but feel a warmth spread through me, but it doesn't completely resolve my doubts.

"I like you too. But I can't help wondering if this is just a temporary escape for both of us."

I dislike being this vulnerable, yet I need more conviction after how he made love to me. His eyes search mine.

"Maybe it started as one, but not now. Not for me. We won't know unless we give it a chance, okay?"

His head dips, and his lips gently brush against mine, teasing and tormenting, until his tongue licks my bottom lip. He boldly plunges inside, igniting a passionate kiss that leaves us both breathless and silences my doubts.

"Okay," I murmur against his lips as his sated cock slips out. "I guess that means we are done."

He laughs and nips at my neck in retaliation—enough to chase away the seriousness and light enough not to leave any marks. My hand drifts over his back to the curve of his ass, where I give it a hard pinch. He rolls off me, howling in pain and grabbing his red cheek. I use his temporary distraction to scoot to the edge of the bed and get off.

"Why did you do that?"

Astonishment covers his face while he twists to see the damage I've done.

"You left these." I point to the matching hickeys adorning my chest. "I thought it only fair to leave my mark."

While I walk into his bathroom to clean up before going home, he bolts from the bed to stare at his butt in the mirror. The used condom dangles, forgotten from his flatulent cock while he studies his flesh. That ass is so high and tight from years of athletics that a simple pinch can't be that big of a deal.

"That hurt."

From the sound of the high pitch of his voice, it seems it's more his pride than physical pain that hurts him. I slip into the water closet to go to the bathroom and wipe down the remnants of us. Behind the closed door, he's muttering something in Italian and making a lot of racket. When I finish and exit to wash my hands, he's standing naked, fiddling with a camera.

"What's that for?"

My curiosity is piqued even though I need to get going since I'm well past the two-hour limit I set.

"For me."

He raises the camera, adjusts the lens, and it clicks. The sound causes my heart to race when I realize he's taking nude pictures of me.

"What the hell do you think you're doing?"

I charge at him with wet hands, prepared to grab the camera when his face suddenly contorts in shock.

"Mia cara? What is wrong?" he asks, lowering the lens he's looking through.

"You're taking pictures of me nude," I state the obvious when I really shouldn't have to. I can't believe his audacity. "Delete it."

His head tilts, but he doesn't move to delete the picture.

Frustration boils within me, and without a second thought, I attempt to snatch his camera away. However, he raises it above my head and out of my reach, causing me to storm angrily into the bedroom.

"Taylor."

I ignore him as I rage, grab my clothes, and tug them on when he touches my elbow.

"Why are you angry at me?"

"Why? Because I didn't consent for you to take naked pictures of me, and you won't delete them."

I whirl around to face him, the camera innocently sitting on the bathroom counter. I could dash to it and smash it into a million pieces, but even I can tell it's expensive.

His hand lingers on my skin, but when I forcefully rip it away, he sighs and walks back to the camera to retrieve it. He opens the viewer, moves in close, and shows me a few that he snapped.

What I don't expect is how good they are. The way the sunlight cascades across my tousled bed hair, picking up the amber highlights in my dark curls. The glow of my skin as the side profile of my arm blocks my breasts and my pussy is blocked by the outline of my thigh.

My expression is relaxed, free of the worries that have plagued me for as long as I can remember. There's an undeniable beauty in the candid shots he took.

"You're beautiful."

As I stare at the images, conflicting emotions come over me. I initially felt violated, but now I can see the intention behind his actions. He wanted to capture a moment of genuine serenity and comfort in my own skin—a side of me usually shrouded in doubts and insecurities.

"I knew I'd remember it in here." He points to his head when I gaze into those chocolate irises. "But I wanted to remember in here too."

He raises the camera with a nervous look.

"Forgive me if I crossed a line."

He reaches for my hand, cups it gently beneath his camera, and then releases it.

"If you want to delete them, I completely understand."

Not that I would know how to delete them, and I'm sure he'd show me if I asked. However, I want to capture what I am looking at now—a gorgeous man who seems to appreciate my body more than I do. I could learn this from him, as he doesn't see my flaws, only my attributes.

"I want to return the favor."

As I lift the camera, I'm struck by the vision before me. His long brown hair frames his masculine features, cascading in unruly waves that give him a rugged charm and accentuate the chiseled contours of his face. His dark chocolate eyes hold a depth of emotion, and a slight smile plays on his lips, reflecting his genuine and kind nature.

I quickly snap two pictures and then turn the viewer around for him to see, but he doesn't glance at the images when he takes the camera from me. Instead, he pulls me closer, wrapping an arm around my waist, and tickles my ribs. I burst out laughing, the sound filling the room. His smile widens as he lowers his lips to mine, capturing my chuckles in a sweet and unexpected kiss.

The camera clicks non-stop, capturing the candid moments of our playful antics, preserving our fun and happiness in a series of spontaneous snapshots. He doesn't bother to show me those pictures when he closes the viewer and sets the camera on his bedside table.

"I don't want you to go," he says in a serious tone. I sigh— the reality of the dreaded Sunday Funday Killer descending upon both of us.

"Me neither," I admit with a longing look, "but I have work to get done and stuff to prepare for tomorrow."

"I know."

He juts out his lower lip to drive his point home, and I chuckle while walking over to retrieve the last of my clothes. He does the same, dressing side by side and stealing occasional glances like we did last night. Reluctantly, I gather my things and walk to his front door. He pulls me close for one last lingering kiss, his lips warm and tender against mine.

"Thank you for this incredible weekend, Taylor. You're truly amazing."

My heart flutters at his words, and I caress his cheek.

"No, thank you. It's been unforgettable. I'll text you when I get home, and we'll plan our next date."

His eyes light up, and he smiles before he releases me.

"I'll be waiting."

Driving back to my high-rise apartment, I can't help but reflect on the incredible weekend we shared. It was unexpected, thrilling, and filled with a connection I hadn't anticipated. Seeing Paolo again fills me with happy excitement, and I can't wait to explore where this newfound relationship might lead.

11

TAYLOR

Monday morning arrives with impending doom as I walk through the bustling hallways toward my beloved corner office. The weekend with Paolo feels like a distant dream, replaced by the harsh reality of the workweek ahead. Chloe intercepts me as I'm lost in thought and worrying if my presentation will be good enough.

"Taylor!" she calls out urgently, her face pulled tight as she barrels down the hall as fast as her stilettos can carry her.

Her impossible good looks and toothpick frame garner attention from passing colleagues she ignores. She tosses her thick blond hair over her shoulder and bustles toward me with a cup of coffee. I stop in my tracks, bracing myself for whatever news she's about to deliver.

"What's going on, Chloe?"

"First off, here. It's your favorite pumpkin crap. I figured you might need this to calm your nerves."

She shoves the piping hot cup into my hand, and I couldn't be more grateful. I didn't have time to grab my usual liquid courage this morning as I wanted to rehearse my presentation as much as possible.

"Or hype you up. I don't know which you want right now."

"I don't know either."

I let out a weary sigh, feeling utterly exhausted after trying to wrap up my presentation. Instead of focusing solely on my work, I traded far too many text messages with Paolo after leaving his place to be efficient in getting my tasks done. He was a welcome distraction.

"I came to warn you. It's a full house in there." She takes a deep breath, her words rushed.

Worry creases her forehead, and if she knew that, she'd immediately dash off to her Botox injector.

"Already?" I glance at my Cartier watch. "The meeting doesn't start for another half hour."

"I don't know," Chloe replies while she scans the hallway for anyone eavesdropping on our conversation. "But I saw a bunch of the directors heading into the conference room. Mr. Williamson seemed pretty chummy with some young guy. They were shaking hands and talking about people they know."

"Who's the young guy?" I ask, my curiosity piqued as I thought it would be management only. Hearing that board members and others are in there makes my heart race.

"Could he be from Jacobsen & Associates? Or maybe that new guy in risk management they hired when I was in Pittsburg? I never got his name or saw his resume. Someone at the top insisted on him."

"Maybe?" She shrugs and breaks into a mischievous smile. "Oh, and he has an accent."

"An accent?" I echo, looking past her to the conference room door firmly closed at the opposite end of the long hallway.

"Yeah, French or maybe Spanish. You know I'm not good at figuring out which is which, but he's very handsome, tall, and with that accent, I'd mount him," she says with a wink.

I chuckle at Chloe's candidness, momentarily easing the mood despite the impending storm brewing in that conference room.

"Well, now you've got me intrigued. I'll figure out who this mysterious accent guy is later," I say, the heat from my latte penetrating my hand. "But I need to run so I can review my presentation one last time and prepare for the meeting. "

Her expression turns serious when she pats my shoulder.

"You've got this, Taylor. Knock 'em dead in there."

"Thanks for the encouragement and the latte."

I lift it in the air as a salute and head toward my office. I want to be as prepared as possible for this meeting. There's no room for error when salvaging the Jacobsen & Associates relationship.

I've reviewed the slide deck so many times that I have mostly memorized it. I sent the final version to Mr. Williamson's secretary late last night. It's one less thing to worry about as I aim for a calm morning and a clear mind to present all the fuckups from Jimothy.

Hopefully, my work digging through the client's transactional activities will be sufficient to get that snake canned when he returns from vacation. It's wishful thinking but a humorous notion that kept me going as I combed through the tedious and often boring trading activity.

There's a tap at my door, and I jolt in my chair, turning to see his secretary delivering the news that they're ready a little earlier than expected. Nervousness churns in my stomach, though not because of the prospect of presenting to the Chairman and a few board members—I've done that many times before.

No, the severity of the situation for the client has me on edge, and the weight of what that means for them. I'm uncertain how to turn this situation around, and I wonder if it might not be my problem to solve once I advise them of what I've found.

"I'll be right there," I respond confidently, though it conflicts with the sudden sweat that coats my body, causing my blouse to stick to my armpits. Thankfully, I'm wearing my black power suit, which hides everything.

I take a deep breath and steady my nerves as I gather my portfolio and latte. I make my way to the conference room, my heels clicking on the polished floor. My mind races with the upcoming presentation and lasting hope that we can salvage this client relationship.

As I push open the conference room door, the atmosphere inside is tense and serious, with all eyes fixed on me. Mr. Williamson stands from his seat at the head of the table and gestures for me to take the empty one beside him. I recognize several board members and offer a respectful nod of acknowledgment as I make my way to the chair while locking onto a pair of captivating chocolate eyes at the other end of the table.

I step back in utter shock, my coffee sloshing in my cup and almost burning my hand. My heart races into my throat, pounding with such intensity that I can feel it reverberating through my body. It's as if it wants to break free from its confines. My breath catches, and I struggle to draw in each inhalation.

Paolo

He raises an eyebrow ever so slightly, a silent acknowledgment that we know each other. He's unwilling to betray our connection, not in front of the board members and executives in this room. I nod imperceptibly in response.

A thousand questions whirl through my mind like a tornado, each adding to the mounting confusion and anxiety that courses through me. How is he here? Why is he here? How in the world did he end up in my office? In my meeting, as if he should be here?

The more I try to make sense of the situation, the less it seems to add up. It's as though the rules of my carefully structured world have been upended, and I'm left grappling with the uncertainty.

Paolo's presence here, in my office, at my workplace, in this critically important meeting—it's all so overwhelming, and I'm struggling to understand it.

As I take my seat beside Mr. Williamson, my heart beats erratically. The room is suffocating. The temperature seems a thousand degrees despite my clammy palms. A subtle tremor runs through my fingers as I clutch the portfolio containing my presentation materials.

I try to focus on Mr. Williamson as he begins the meeting, but my eyes drift back to Paolo as if staring at him will make sense of why he's here. Our eyes lock for a moment until his jaw clenches, and his gaze flickers back to Mr. Williamson's introduction of me and the purpose of my presentation.

My breaths come faster, shallow and anxious, as I desperately try to maintain a facade of composure. This is not how I imagined or prepared for this meeting to go. A heavy dread coils in my stomach, threatening to consume me entirely.

I slowly rise from my seat, my fingertips pressing into the polished table as Mr. Williamson yields the floor to me. Every step feels like a monumental effort, and my legs wobble slightly as I approach the podium at the front of the room. Everyone's eyes on me intensify my anxiety. I can't shake the feeling that this presentation will be far more challenging than any I've faced before.

With a deep breath that I hope conceals my unease, I begin. The clicker in my hand feels almost foreign as I advance through the slides, my voice projecting with practiced confidence. But inside, I'm a turbulent sea of emotions, my thoughts often straying to Paolo and flashes of this weekend.

As I delve into the details of the client's investments and

their trading activities, my gaze occasionally meets his. Our eyes lock for brief moments, exchanging unspoken messages that only deepen the intrigue and confusion of the situation. I can see curiosity and concern in his chocolate irises, mirroring my turmoil.

Despite the distractions, I push through the presentation, determined to do justice to the seriousness of the situation. I'm bombarded with questions, disputes between different parties in the room, and having to backtrack through the trades to explain where and how they took place. At some point, the concerns for the client's relationship take over, and I'm able to ignore Paolo completely as he quietly observes.

The meeting stretches on, the intensity of the discussions showing no signs of abating. I'm determined to leave no stone unturned in addressing the situation while ensuring the firm's reputation remains intact. Only when the room finally starts to settle, with decisions and action plans being made, do I allow myself a moment to steal a glance at Paolo, who gives me an impressed nod that doesn't go unnoticed by Mr. Williamson when I return to my seat.

When the meeting finally adjourns, I take my cold coffee and notes and escape the confines of the conference room as fast as I can to dart into the ladies' room. Needing a confidante, I pull my phone out of my portfolio pocket and dial Chloe's number, hoping she's at her desk and available to talk.

"Chloe, it's me," I say urgently as she answers my call on the first ring. "I need you to come to the ladies' room right away. Something unexpected just happened, and I don't know how to handle it."

"Are you okay? Did you get sick? Did you get your period?" Chloe's voice has a hint of concern as she responds.

"None of that. Just get in here."

"I'm on my way."

She slams the phone down. Two minutes later, I hear her

running stilettos pound on the floor outside until she pushes through the door.

"Taylor, what's wrong?"

I dump all my stuff on the counter and check the stalls to ensure we are alone before I whirl around to tell Chloe about Paolo.

"That guy in there? The handsome one with the accent?"

Her eyes dance as she leans closer, awaiting the drama she suspects is coming.

"I know him."

Her expression falters a fraction when her eyes narrow.

"What do you mean you know him?"

"Well, I haven't had a chance to tell you, but I sort of had a thing with him . . . this weekend."

She gasps, and her eyes grow wide with surprise.

"Noooooo."

The restroom suddenly feels like a confessional booth as I continue, "Yes, and I asked him out. Like to keep seeing him."

She shakes her head, tossing a thumb over her shoulder.

"But he's here. In your meeting with all the big boys?"

"I know."

I take a deep breath and explain the bizarre turn of events that unfolded from the bakery to Paolo's unexpected presence at the meeting.

"This is so weird," she finally remarks. "And you didn't know him before this? I mean, I've never seen him before either, and with a face like that, I'd remember."

I cast her a serious expression.

"Trust me, if I recognized him at the bakery, it wouldn't have led where it did."

"What are you going do to?" she whispers when the door suddenly swings open to a colleague needing to use the facilities.

We quickly turn toward the mirror, her to fix her make-up

and me to collect my cup and portfolio. I shake my head, equally puzzled.

"The only thing I can do is go back to work. Management agreed on an action plan for the client, and I must turn over my findings to some forensic accounting person to validate before we take this any further," I murmur as my phone buzzes with a message. I glance at it briefly and see Paolo's name on the screen, but I quickly tuck it into my portfolio, out of Chloe's sight.

"While you're doing that, I'm going to ask around and find out more about him and what he's doing here," she says, pulling open the door for us to whisper in the hallway.

I appreciate Chloe's offer to help uncover more about Paolo's presence at our company.

"That's a good idea. See what you can dig up, but be discreet about it."

"Will do."

We part ways, going opposite directions down the hallway until I reach the glass door of my office and swing it closed. This is one of many times I wish I didn't have a wall of windows looking into my office so I could hide from people. Or just one person in particular. Paolo.

I sink into my leather chair behind my desk, trying to gather my thoughts, when his text message nags at me. Succumbing to my curiosity, I relent and read it.

> Taylor, we need to talk.
>
> Come to lunch with me.

Then I realize.
He lied.
Then made love to me.

12

PAOLO

Walking into that meeting room this morning, I could never have imagined the tumultuous storm engulfing me. My stomach churns with guilt, threatening to spew the breakfast I had with my father before arriving here. I purposely didn't tell her yesterday. The consequences of my deceit hang over my head, causing my chest to tighten.

She's the last one in the room. A vision in her black suit exudes an aura of professionalism and confidence. Her dark hair frames her face with elegance, and her green eyes are a striking contrast.

I can't help but notice the subtle paling of her complexion when her eyes fall on me—a fleeting flicker of surprise, panic, and fear. It's a reaction I should've expected but fervently hoped would be different. Guilt grips me as I realize the depth of my betrayal when her gaze strays to mine several times while Ted talks.

During her presentation, I watch as she expertly navigates through the intricate details of the trades, her voice unwavering and resolute. Yet, her eyes, assertive and commanding, purposefully avoid me as much as possible. She only glances in my direction when necessary, and even then, her gaze is fleeting, refusing to linger.

The subsequent meeting is equally challenging for me, trapped in a torturous position between loyalty to my father and my temporary employer and my developing feelings for Taylor. I barely hear the conversation swirling around me, even when things escalate between the board members as my thoughts remain with Taylor.

I can't shake the image of her pale face when she first saw me. The way her green eyes darted away, avoiding me as much as possible during the presentation. It starkly contrasts with the vibrant woman I spent the weekend with, who was full of life and passion.

Regret gnaws at me, knowing I should've been honest with her yesterday. My reasons for not telling her were utterly selfish. Seeing how her hand trembled and the distress she did well in hiding lets me know I made the wrong choice. Perhaps I can make amends and resolve the betrayal I caused. I sneak my phone under the table and text her an invitation to lunch to talk and clear up this mess.

My father's stern voice snaps me back to the meeting, and I force myself to focus on the matters at hand. My phone remains frustratingly silent throughout the meeting, and the longer it drags on, the more my hope of hearing from Taylor dwindles. I can't help but steal glances at the device, hoping to see her name flash on the screen with a message. As time ticks on and no response from her, I become increasingly anxious. With each passing minute, I wonder if she'll ever speak to me again, let alone go to lunch.

As the meeting concludes, I'm dejected and worried. I want to rectify things with her, but it won't be easy. Rebuilding the trust I've shattered will take time and effort, both of which I'm willing to do if she gives me the chance.

I leave the meeting room while my father and Ted continue conversing about my assignment with the company. Their words are a distant hum in my ears as I pull out my phone and send another text message to Taylor. Intending to get an answer from her, I walk away from them to call her. Before it can connect, my father claps me on the back and guides me toward Ted.

"Paolo, we've got a lot of work ahead of us with this discovery," Ted says in a serious tone that has my father releasing my shoulder and clenching his teeth. "We'll need you to work closely with Taylor Woods. It's high time for introductions. Let's all go to lunch together to iron out the details."

I quickly pocket my phone, trying to conceal the dread settling over me. After hearing the details in her presentation, it's far more complex than I initially expected and hints at a cover-up. I'd usually jump at the chance to work on it, yet working closely with Taylor on it is the last thing I want to do. This is stepping into her territory and into the very 'boys club' mentality she despises. I'd much prefer to work on it alone, if possible. Or not at all.

"Excellent, lead the way," I force myself to say with feigned enthusiasm, something my father immediately picks up on. However, I admit to nothing as Ted takes the lead, guiding us to her office.

"What is that about?" my father mutters under his breath, clearly puzzled, and I shake my head. No way in hell am I divulging my proclivities to my father. He didn't know about my ex and he won't find out about Taylor. I quicken my pace, catching up with Ted to avoid my father.

"Where would you like me to set up? Do you have a private office, preferably on another floor? Somewhere away from curious workers?"

As we walk past a row of glass offices, I notice that my presence is already drawing a few curious looks, especially from a slender blonde who gives me a familiar smile, even though we're strangers.

Ted considers my question momentarily before responding, "Actually, I think it would be beneficial for you to work here on the ninth floor next to Taylor. It will make communication and collaboration with her much easier. Let's use this office."

He points to an empty office with a view of the city skyline. It would be nice if I weren't preoccupied with staring at Taylor in her office, where she's frowning at her phone. Feeling my gaze, her head darts up, and our eyes lock. Hers narrow at the same time a scowl tightens her full lips, but her expression quickly shifts into something more friendly as she waves to my father beside me.

Ted hollers for her to come out and meet her new colleague. She stands, her actions calculated as she tugs on the hem of her jacket, a subtle display of power, before confidently crossing the room. There's a veiled threat in her eyes. A silent message that she's not pleased with my earlier deception.

"Paolo Cavallaro, this is Taylor Woods. She's single-handedly constructed this report over this past weekend. Worked day and night to compile the presentation you saw this morning," Ted says with reverence in his tone.

"Thank you, Mr. Williamson," Taylor responds with a tone that carries an air of professionalism and restraint. Her eyes briefly flicker toward him, revealing nothing as she extends her hand to me. "It's nice to meet you."

She takes my hand, her grip firm but not unfriendly.

"The pleasure is all mine," I reply, giving her an easy smile while brushing my thumb across the top of her hand. It goes unnoticed by the men beside me as she snatches her hand away as discreetly as possible.

"Well, if you'll excuse me, I must return to work."

She's already taken two steps back before Ted stops her.

"Now that we're all acquainted, let's discuss how we will tackle this situation with Jacobsen & Associates. Taylor, join us for lunch."

She hesitates momentarily. Her gaze darts between Ted and the growing pile of paperwork on her desk. She offers a polite smile.

"I appreciate the offer, Mr. Williamson, but I'm afraid I have a lot of work to catch up on since I had to shift priorities to work on the Jacobsen relationship."

"Nonsense, Taylor. You can bring Paolo up to speed over lunch so he can get started on it immediately, and you can return to your other clients."

Ted seems determined to make this lunch happen. He waves off her excuse with a genial chuckle. Taylor looks torn, but she ultimately relents with a polite nod.

"Alright, Mr. Williamson, if you insist. Let me grab my things, and I'll join you at the elevators."

As she turns to gather her belongings, Ted turns to my father.

"Will you be joining us?"

My father's eyes linger on me and then flicker to Taylor as if trying to determine our possible connection.

"My father has business elsewhere to attend to," I reply coolly on his behalf. He needs to leave to prevent the situation from becoming even more uncomfortable than it already is.

As if my response snaps his attention back to the conversation, he says, "Yes, of course. Paolo, I will call you later. Perhaps you could stop by for dinner with your mother sometime."

"Of course."

I give a subtle nod, noticing Taylor's eyes narrowing as she observes our brief interaction and could be scheming to use it against me when we have a chance to talk privately.

"I'll walk you out," Ted offers, taking my father aside and

leading him toward the exit. As they walk away, my stomach hardens. Without hesitation, I dart into Taylor's office, closing the glass door gently behind me.

"Taylor," I implore in a hushed tone, anxiety coursing through me. "We need to talk."

"No, Paolo. There's nothing you can say that will excuse this. You knew yesterday, held me as I went on and on about it, and intentionally kept quiet. It's absolutely inexcusable."

Her hands tremble with anger as I step closer. Her face is a mask of cool confidence directed toward the glass wall of the office. Mine carries an open humility as I turn away from the rest of the office to focus solely on her.

"I know," I admit, pouring all my guilt and regret into my voice. "I messed up and should've been honest from the beginning. I'm truly sorry for what I did, and I understand you're angry. But please, let me explain."

"Mr. Williamson is waiting on us. I don't want to—"

"He can wait," I cut her off, urgency pushing me forward. "I need to make this right, Taylor. What I did was wrong, and I never wanted to hurt you."

"You should have thought about that before you lied," she retorts in anger but the underlining hurt rims her words.

She stomps around me, intent on leaving the room. I instinctively follow until she spins around, seething inches from my face.

"And you know the worst part about it all," she continues, her voice filled with bitterness. "You made love to me as if it meant something. What a fool I was to believe the sweet words of some kid."

Her words hit their intended mark, hurting me as profoundly as I hurt her. I gently touch her arm, my voice soft and filled with remorse.

"It meant something—more than you know. I just . . . I didn't handle it correctly, and I'm so sorry."

"It doesn't matter. You were just a weekend fling."

She turns away, rips open the door, and walks out of the room, leaving me utterly gutted.

"It's more than a fling."

13

TAYLOR

"Paolo, is it?"

I keep my tone neutral as I gaze at him for the first time since he helped me out of the back of the stifling car services we took to the restaurant.

"Tell me how you learned about our firm and its recent situation."

Paolo's eyebrows rise slightly when I act as if I forgot his name. An immature ploy to get back at him, as his lying has made this the most awkward lunch of my career. Fury simmers beneath my calm facade. The tension is undeniable, but he and I put on our best professional faces. Rather than Paolo answering, my boss jumps into the conversation.

"Paolo is an extremely talented young man," Mr. Williamson says with a sly grin, leaning in slightly. "He's an investigator, auditor, and, as you know, a forensic accountant. He's caught quite a bit of corporate corruption in his brief career. Tell her about the Ponzi scheme you uncovered before joining our firm."

I nod, annoyed by the compliments pouring out of Mr.

Williamson's mouth, as I've never heard any accolades directed my way after all the years I've worked for the firm. I went from being ignored and unheard to being thrust front and center into a potential scandal for our company if it were to get leaked to the press. It's a sudden shift that leaves me feeling uneasy and strangely empowered.

Paolo glances at Mr. Williamson, gulping uncomfortably, and then back at me as he chooses his words carefully.

"I've worked on various cases, but my focus is on situations where confidentiality and discretion are paramount. It involves the run-of-the-mill corporate matters, such as unethical behaviors and practices, insider trading, embezzlement, whistleblowing, and yes, most recently, a Ponzi scheme."

It's impressive. I can't deny that. Yet beneath the surface, every word, look, and gesture Paolo directs at me carries a sense of betrayal. He knew the truth and could have told me, yet he chose not to. That fact continues to play on a loop in my brain, a constant reminder of his deception.

I do my best to focus on the conversation, determined to stay in the present. I push aside the pitiful look on Paolo's face, refusing to let it occupy my thoughts. Despite the compliments and accolades he receives, a layer of distrust settles between us, making it hard to fully engage in the lunch meeting.

"So, they discreetly brought you in to investigate Jacobsen & Associates?"

The puzzle pieces fall into place, and my eyes widen with realization.

Paolo nods slowly.

"Yes, that's correct."

Mr. Williamson interjects, adding his perspective, "Paolo's expertise will be instrumental in helping us navigate this delicate situation, Taylor. Jacobsen is closely connected with some high-profile individuals in town, not to mention a couple of board members. It's why we need to jump on this immediately, and with Paolo's assistance, we should have this put to bed this week."

As I sip my drink, the atmosphere becomes charged with unspoken tension. I can feel Paolo's gaze on me, and I'm sure he's bracing himself for my reaction. It is a *delicate situation* indeed, and I need a moment to process everything. If they called him to handle it, I could turn over the findings to him and wash my hands of this mess. Wash my hands of Paolo too. Sounds perfect to me. After a pause, I change the subject.

"Mr. Williamson, you mentioned that Jacobsen & Associates has a close relationship with the board of directors. How does that affect this?"

Mr. Williamson leans back in his chair with an enigmatic smile.

"Ah, yes. Well, you may find this interesting. Paolo's father is also on the board of directors at Jacobsen & Associates."

On the board of both companies? The revelation hits me like a tidal wave, and I realize I had overlooked a crucial connection when Paolo was introduced earlier. The shock of seeing him sitting in my meeting came first, and now, everything makes sense. It's the boys club and networking of connections that made this happen. One of the things I complained to him about, and he's directly a part of and benefiting from it. It heightens my anger and makes it hard to sit through the remainder of this lunch.

"I see. That's . . . quite the connection."

Paolo's discomfort is evident when he grabs his water glass and downs it in one drink. If it were yesterday, I'd feel terrible and reach out to him. But now, after learning the truth about his role in this situation and his deception, he deserves every awkward and uncomfortable feeling.

Despite the emotional turmoil brewing within me at each new revelation, I remain composed, my professional facade firmly in place as I glare at both men. I continue to steer the conversation, digging deeper into the details of the situation, while Paolo sits there, appearing increasingly upset and conflicted.

As lunch progresses, he slumps in his chair and picks at his food, which is a small vindication on my part. Deep down, I hope he's miserable and suffering as much as I am.

Everything is going fine until Mr. Williamson's phone suddenly rings, and he grabs it. He wipes his mouth quickly, placing his napkin next to his half-eaten lunch to grumble into his phone.

"I've got to head back," he says, his tone turning serious. "I'll send the car back for you both after it drops me off."

Paolo and I exchange glances, both aware of the awkwardness that has taken over the situation. My boss stands, as does Paolo, out of respect for his family's friend while I remain seated.

"Uh, we can come too. We're done here anyway, correct?" I ask my boss because I don't want to sit alone with Paolo. It gives him too much control and leverage to hold me captive as he blabbers on with more apologies—something I can't and won't listen to.

"No, Taylor. Stay and get to know each other. This will probably be your last relaxed meal this week," he says without considering my objections.

Relaxed is the last thing this meal will be when he leaves. I may just stab Paolo with my fork. That would definitely get me out of working with him on this project.

"We'll stay," Paolo says, stuffing his hands in his pockets.

"Good," Mr. Williamson says, tucking his phone in his pocket before eyeing both of us. "I want an update this afternoon."

"From Paolo?"

I need to clarify as I have a mountain of other work to get

done, and I'm eager to hand this off to the board's nepotism hire. A strange look crosses over both their faces, leaving me curious, but I'm undeterred. I want off of this project. I didn't want to do it when I found out it was Jimothy's failure, and I certainly don't want to work on it with Paolo involved.

"From the both of you. You'll be working together on this project, Taylor. I thought I made that clear. He'll lead the way with his expertise, and you'll handle the client communication and solution presentation," Mr. Williamson reiterates in annoyance.

My blood crawls in my veins, and I resist the urge to pull on my earlobes, struggling to accept what I'm hearing. Paolo's intense gaze bores into mine, and I am trapped in the silent exchange of looks between him and my boss.

"Mr. Williamson, that's not necessary," I protest, my voice determined. "With his experience, he's far more qualified to handle these situations and would be a better candidate to discuss the intricacies with Mr. Jacobsen."

I rise to my feet, my body tense with resistance and unwilling to accept his decision. Mr. Williamson's expression remains firm as he glares at me.

"Taylor, this is not up for negotiation. I've made my decision, and I expect both of you to cooperate and deliver results."

Paolo's gaze remains on me. His eyes reflect a mix of emotions I can't quite decipher. It's clear that he's not thrilled about this arrangement either, but he remains silent, letting my boss's words ring with finality. Reluctantly, I nod, realizing that arguing further won't change the outcome.

"Understood, Mr. Williamson. We'll do our best to make this partnership work."

My boss nods in approval, and I see a hint of satisfaction in his eyes. With that, he heads for the exit, leaving Paolo and me alone at the table. I collapse into my chair, disgusted, frustrated, and angry at our unwanted collaboration.

Luckily, Paolo doesn't say anything else when he sinks into his chair across from me. We both sit in silence for what feels like an eternity. My appetite has vanished, and it seems Paolo's has as well when he pushes his mostly full plate away from him and leans closer to me.

"Taylor," he begins, his voice carrying that distinctive rolling 'r' that used to be so enticing, but I immediately quell any romantic notions.

"Don't even start, Paolo. I'm not happy about this, and I'm not happy with you."

It sounds juvenile, but it's the most restrained way to express my frustration in this crowded upscale restaurant.

"I know I deserve all this and more, but I didn't have a chance to explain yesterday." His chocolate eyes are deep rivers of guilt and worry. "Can we somehow set aside 'us' for now? You can hate me for this week, and then—"

I cut him off, my tone unyielding.

"Let's make one thing clear, Paolo. I won't forget what you did, but I'll do my best to cooperate on this project because it's my livelihood on the line. I don't float and flitter from job to job that my dad lines up for me."

More juvenile words spew from me, intending to hurt him as he hurt me. When his jaw clenches, I go in for the kill.

"But after it's over, we go back to being strangers. Is that understood?"

He nods, regret and understanding crossing his handsome face.

"Of course."

He runs a hand through his hair, tucking it behind his ears. I was wrong. Apparently, you can have long hair in corporate America if you are the son of a multimillionaire father who sits on the board of a valuable investment house and its VIP client. I'm sure there's a conflict of interest some-where in all this, but I'm not about to stick my neck out and report someone in the boys' club, regardless of how much I want to.

We're bound together in this for now, but I'm determined not to let it affect my professionalism or ability to do a good job. After this week, he'll be out of my company and my life forever. That thought brings the first genuine smile to my face on this otherwise awful day.

14

TAYLOR

The car ride back to the office is painfully awkward. We both sit in silence, avoiding eye contact, with me staring out the window the entire time. When we reach the office building, I practically sprint to the elevators to prevent sharing the confined space with him, desperate to put as much distance as possible between us.

I settle into my desk, determined to focus on the project at hand. I know I can't afford any distractions, especially with the Jacobsen & Associates account on the line. I quickly prioritize my tasks, deciding to knock out some work for my other clients that will have to take a backseat this week.

I find solace in the routine tasks and my mood lifts. Just as I find the rhythm in my work, Chloe bustles into my office, her eyes wide with curiosity.

"What happened? I saw you storm out of here with him following like a kicked puppy," she asks, perching herself on the edge of my desk. "The whole office is buzzing about it, especially since he's right there."

She points to our joined walls when she lowers her voice. I've sat by that empty office for so long I hadn't considered that

I'd also need to lower my voice. I sigh inwardly, not in the mood for this added complexity of guarding my speaking volume.

"What's everyone saying?"

Despite my determination to focus on work, I can't help but be curious. If there's already office gossip about me and Paolo, I want to know. It's my job on the line if anyone suspects our involvement.

Chloe leans in closer as if sharing classified information. "Well, some wonder who he is and what he's doing here."

"That's fair," I murmur, turning my cell phone face down when a message from Paolo appears on my screen requesting to talk to me.

"Others wonder what Mr. Williamson's doing on the floor and with all the board members here. You know how everyone talks when they're around."

Another fair observation. They rarely use the conference room down here, preferring to use the larger, fancier one outside the Chairman's office.

"Does anyone suspect it's a client issue?"

Her expression turns serious when she asks, "No, should they?"

If we lose Jacobsen, it's not just about the revenue we stand to lose from that account. It's a reputation risk and sends a message to our other clients. They might start questioning our stability and jump ship. It could snowball into a mass exodus, and the company might not recover.

"No, they shouldn't, so we must keep this under wraps."

She closes her lips and twists as if locking them, tossing the imaginary key over her shoulder.

"Done. Now, can we talk about what *you* are going to do? Obviously, he's working here, but for how long? And does this have anything to do with you both leaving with Mr. Williamson?"

"We're working on a project together. That's it."

She raises an eyebrow skeptically.

"Come on, Taylor. I heard from Mr. Williamson's assistant that he practically ran into his office, and then you two appeared later. Something's up."

My gaze turns distant, wondering if there is something bigger going on. It was odd how quickly he left the restaurant. I was too preoccupied with being alone with Paolo to have dwelled on it. Now that I am away from him and have a clearer mind, I'm curious what makes the Chairman of the Board leave anywhere so abruptly.

"I only know what I know. And even that's not much at this point."

I shrug, not knowing what else to say but feeling a stress headache brewing above my eyes. I dig around in my desk drawer for some pain relievers under her watchful eye, hoping she drops the conspiracy theory I don't have time to entertain.

"I'm getting a headache."

"Well, I'll let you get back to work," she says, gazing at me as I down the pills. "Call me if you need anything. Otherwise, I'll stare at your boy as his office is diagonal to mine."

"He's not my anything," I defend, but it's too late as Paolo chooses that exact moment to enter my office.

Chloe slides off my desk to make introductions with him, and I can't help but feel my frustration rising for the millionth time today. His eyes briefly flicker past her to linger on me when he shakes her hand. I know that with both of their interruptions, I won't be getting much done today. It looks like another late night at the office.

She flashes me a sneaky smile behind his back when she leaves. He strides into my office, a stack of documents in his hand. His expression is one of focused intensity as he approaches my desk.

"I've been going through the trades and the entries," he begins as he sits in the guest chair opposite my desk. "I have a few questions about some of the companies and transactions. Do you have a moment?"

I nod, intrigued by his thoroughness.

"Of course. What do you need to know?"

As he starts asking about specific entries and companies, I can't help but be impressed by his attention to detail and the intelligent questions he poses. His knowledge of financial matters is evident, and I find myself listening intently, forgetting for a moment the awkwardness that has plagued us since lunch.

But then, as we discuss a particular trade, his gaze drops, and I feel a strange heat wash over me. He's staring at my lips, and I can't deny the magnetic pull between us. Time seems to stand still as we share an intimate moment. Paolo blinks as if shaking himself out of a trance and clears his throat.

"I'm sorry. I got lost in thought for a second."

I swallow hard, my heart pounding in my chest. "It's . . . it's okay."

We return to the task at hand, but the atmosphere in my office changes. The professional facade we both wear is beginning to crack, and I can't help but feel that spark of physical attraction to him. I shove my desire away, laughing at his joke and watching the relief erase his serious expression. When he's content with sufficient answers to his questions, he leaves, and I return to work on my other clients.

Hours pass, my headache remains, and my update to Mr. Williamson is on his desk. It's only when Chloe waves goodbye that I glance out the window. The sun dips below the horizon, casting long shadows across the cityscape. It's well into the early evening, and the office has quieted. I order dinner while continuing to work.

As I go to Paolo's office to ask him a question, my steps slow when I see his dark office. He's already left for the day, leaving me irritated. Given the importance of our project and the looming deadline, I expected him to be working late as well. My anger sparks right back up to high as I take my frustrations out by pounding away on my keyboard until security rings my line advising of my dinner delivery.

It's disheartening to find myself the only one working late, especially when I expected him to be equally dedicated to the project. Boy, was I wrong.

The next two days pass with him being absent from the office and I'm left to grapple with a whirlwind of emotions. Anger and frustration dominate, but beneath it all lies a hint of worry that I can't entirely ignore. Chloe's frequent visits to my office only amplify my concern as she asks the same questions circling my mind.

Despite his physical absence, my inbox is inundated with emails from him. Each message contains a detailed summary of why he's requesting information, and it becomes clear that the trades extend farther back than we initially identified. We divide the work, with me taking the current year and him taking the prior years.

The workload is demanding, and the pressure to uncover the truth about these trades is relentless. With each passing day, I miss Paolo's presence, both in the office and in our collaboration. His dedication to the project is evident in his constant communication, and I can't help but grudgingly admire his work ethic.

What surprises me the most is the timing of his messages. Late into the night, my inbox lights up with emails and voice messages from Paolo, each containing new discoveries and theories. He's as much of a workaholic as I am, if not more. The relentless pursuit for answers keeps him burning the midnight oil, just as it does me.

A strange camaraderie develops between us, and I question my initial anger and resentment for his betrayal. Perhaps there's more to Paolo than I had initially assumed. As the days turn into nights, and the project consumes my every waking moment, I can't help but wonder if I should talk to him and iron this out. Could I be missing out on something great because of one huge omission?

By Thursday morning, I'm freaking out with his absence. We must present everything we've been working on and all possible solutions to Mr. Williamson tomorrow, and he's still not in the office.

With each passing minute, my worry intensifies. The questions and concerns swirl in my mind. Where could Paolo be? Is he alright? Has something happened that's preventing him from being here? Or is this deliberate? Another twist in this complex entanglement between us?

The clock ticks relentlessly, and I check my email and phone repeatedly, hoping for any sign of communication from Paolo. But the empty inbox and silent phone only amplify my growing concerns. It's like the waterfall of communication from him all week has stopped, and even my phone calls to him are going straight to his voicemail. If I knew someone else to call, I would, but now I'm pacing the floor with worry. Worry for him, his safety, and his wellbeing. Not to mention worry for me, the client presentation, and my overall job.

As the minutes turn into hours, my mind races through all sorts of terrible scenarios, and my stomach burns. Only when I start looking up hospitals in the area do I catch a glimpse of Paolo out of the corner of my eye carrying a box of those damn macarons and a cup of tea.

My heart leaps in my chest. I rush out of my office and into his, seeing him perfectly fine and healthy, about to eat one of those shimmery cookies without a care in the world. I seethe with fury at his inconsideration of my feelings.

"Where the fuck have you been? And why did you go to *our place* to get macarons?"

15

PAOLO

Her dark green eyes glitter dangerously as her hands plant on those curvy hips. The anger in her gaze is unmistakable, and I can't help but smile at her reaction. Given that I didn't think she cared whether I lived or died on Monday, this shift in her attitude is the nicest surprise I could have hoped for.

And if I wasn't mistaken, she said *our place* when referring to the cookies she loves so much. Little does she know, they are a peace offering for how things ended the other day. I was getting her favorite flavors out of the box to hand deliver to her.

Her hair is elegantly pulled back, a wisp escaping to frame her face. The dark waves are artfully twisted into a knot at the top of her head, and exhaustion is etched onto her delicate features. Her blouse gapes as she's missed a button, revealing far too much of her breasts and the remnants of my hickeys—making me proud.

She looks absolutely stunning, and I'd easily bend her over this desk to bury my cock deep inside her. After all the hard work we've put in this week and her bitchy attitude right now, a few orgasms would serve both of us some good. I shift in my chair as my hardening cock agrees.

"Well, good morning to you too, Taylor," I say with a sly grin, fully embracing this feisty version of her that's emerged in contrast to the cold and aloof one from earlier in the week.

It's why I chose to work remotely. We'd likely get a lot more done if I wasn't in her direct proximity. Besides, there's the added benefit of not having to contend with the inconvenient hard on that seems to occur whenever I'm around her, something her observant blonde friend didn't fail to notice.

Not to mention, it helped hiding out at Sebastian's house to lick my wounds in private. I needed to confide in him about what transpired between her and me and get an objective opinion. Or as objective as he can be, given his playboy lifestyle and a strong aversion to being involved with anyone. He still doesn't understand my attraction to older women, but he did say he wanted me to be happy. More specifically, 'If this broad makes you happy, go for it.'

That piece of advice I expected as he supports me in everything I do, even with his lackadaisical attitude about women. I think when he finally falls in love, he'll understand completely. Until then, well, he won't.

"Morning? Morning, Paolo?"

She closes the distance, leaning over my desk and giving me a beautiful view of those full breasts when she points to the time on my computer. My eyes don't bother moving. I couldn't care less about the time as fantasies of motorboating them fill my mind, causing my pants to tighten. She jolts back when she notices where I'm looking, standing straight and realizing the button she missed.

"Oh, grow up."

I shrug, thoroughly amused by her, as I lean back in my chair for her to see the effect she has on me. When her gaze flickers down to the tent in my pants as she fiddles with the button, her eyes narrow, and a scowl slides onto her face. I chuckle. The disdain is obvious, yet I still want her to know how I feel about her. Despite everything that's happened this week, nothing has changed for me. My focus has been on figuring out how I can make it up to her and then carrying out a plan for a second chance.

"Now that we got that out of the way, how can I help you?"

I turn the tables on her by changing my demeanor to that of a dedicated professional as I lean forward to unpack my bag.

"Cut the crap and tell me why I hadn't heard from you all day?"

Her eyes are still blazing, even after covering her breasts, which is a damn shame. Although the thought of every man in here seeing them bothers me. If she's mine, then I'm hers. I don't share with others.

"I missed you too, mia cara," I purr at her, and she crosses the room to close the door.

Unbeknownst to her, the glass is an amplifier to all her conversations. I was happy to hear her tell her friend we're involved. It pleased me greatly and yielded curious looks from the friend the rest of the day.

"Don't even start with me. Our presentation is due tomorrow, and I sent you my part, which you haven't responded to. I've diligently gotten back to you expeditiously, even when I'm in the middle of something else from my regular job. You've never had to wait for me as I've had to wait for you."

Her lips curl up in disapproval, and as much as I enjoy her showy display of anger, I grab the documents from my bag and toss them on the desk toward her.

"See for yourself."

She grabs the papers and starts rifling through them, her eyes glancing up occasionally.

"What is this?"

I watch Taylor's expression. She leans closer to the desk, her eyes wide and her fingers gripping the furniture's edge.

"The trades we've been investigating are not just fraudulent. They're part of a much larger and intricate embezzlement scheme. This morning, I conducted site surveys on the properties and companies involved, and what I found points to a widespread financial deception of alarming proportions."

"But..."

She thumbs through picture after picture, lifting the sticky note I jotted the total amount of trades per property. Her eyebrows raise into her hairline as shock overtakes her face.

"Are you sure, Paolo?"

"Yes, I stayed up late last night, and that's when it struck me to document everything, from irregularities in the financial records to discrepancies in property ownership. It's a well-orchestrated operation, and it goes deep."

"Wait." Her voice trembles as she responds, "This is Jimothy's lake house."

She holds up a picture in one hand and shuffles through the pages on my desk until she finds the county assessor's property records, which list a corporate entity.

"Who's Jimothy?"

Taylor's eyes meet mine, hatred replacing shock—something I've never seen before, even when she was at her angriest with me.

"Jimothy is what I call him because I hate him. His real name is Jim Wraith, Chief Accounting Officer," she says bitterly, pointing to an empty office across the bank of cubicles in front of mine. "And he's so far up the CEO's ass, I doubt he'd even believe us if we were to share this information with him."

"Are you saying what I think you're saying?" I murmur as she hands me the photo and returns to thumbing through my research, scattering it all over my desk as if looking for something else.

She doesn't answer. Her fingers rush around, flipping through pages and occasionally muttering to herself as she scans the information. Her brows furrow with concentration. She's determined to find whatever she's seeking until she stops at a photo of a lavish penthouse. She holds up the picture, her face a mask of confusion.

"How did you get a picture of the inside of this penthouse?"

I look sheepish, realizing I may have to admit to bending the rules a bit. "Well, I may have bribed the security guard to get that photo. I thought it might be relevant to our investigation since a picture of the outside of the high rise wouldn't mean much."

Taylor's eyes widen for a brief moment. "You bribed a security guard? Seriously?"

"Desperate times call for desperate measures, Taylor."

I can't help but grin. My response elicits a smile from her, the first one today. I feel like a superhero getting back on more solid footing with her. Last night, as I hatched the plan, it seemed ridiculous to waste precious time running around town doing site surveys. Watching her connect the dots, I know it's the right move.

Taylor studies the penthouse picture, her eyes narrowing as she scrutinizes every detail. The smile slides from her face until she looks almost sick.

"I'll be right back," she says abruptly, dashing out of my office. The door shuts behind her with a thud, leaving me in suspense.

Moments later, she reappears with her phone in hand. Her fingers tremble when she shows me the screen. The photo is a revelation. I can't blame her for being shaken. The penthouse is listed under one of the shell corporations through which fraudulent trades are funneled.

In the image, Taylor and the blonde woman stand by a lavishly decorated Christmas tree, flanked by none other than

Jim Wraith and Roland Frasier, the Chief Executive Officer of Williamson Cooper. The caption reads: "Holiday celebrations with the CEO and his right-hand man, Jim."

I clutch the picture the security guard obtained and compare the two. The wallpaper, the furnishing, and the view beyond are identical. The realization of what we uncovered makes the hair on the back of my neck stand on end, and an uneasy feeling settles into my gut.

Taylor's voice quivers as she speaks. "Paolo, this is damning evidence. It connects Jimothy and Roland to that penthouse. *Roland's penthouse.* They're in this together."

"Are you sure? Taylor, these are large sums of money, tens of millions over the last decade."

"In recent years, there's been a sudden surge in extravagant vacations, exotic trips like big game hunting in Argentina with their sons, brand new SUVs for Jimothy and Roland and their wives parading around in expensive jewelry and furs every time they are up here. It aligns perfectly with these fraudulent trades. They've been diverting company funds for their own personal indulgences, using fake entities to do it, and this evidence confirms it."

Her eyes race over the pictures while her fingertips rest on a few of them. I continue to examine the incriminating evidence, my heart pounding as Taylor points out the extravagances she's observed over the years. It's a chilling revelation that only someone intimately acquainted with these men and their lifestyle could piece together from her corner office view.

"You're saying that these two executives somehow acquired them for personal use through these different companies and their listed properties? For residential use?"

"It appears so," she answers in a disbelieving tone.

Her fingers skim through the documents as her wide green eyes remain fixed in shock. I can't help but shake my head in disbelief as I absorb the breadth and depth of this investigation.

"This is beyond anything I imagined, Taylor. It's not just embezzlement. It's full-blown fraud, collusion, and conspiracy."

"This can't wait until tomorrow. We need to show this to Mr. Williamson right away."

I offer a reassuring smile. "I couldn't agree more."

I return the phone to her, which she tucks into her suit pocket and helps me gather all the pictures and pages of documentation. Once they are in order, she hands them to me, throws open the door, and glares at Jim's empty office. It doesn't go unnoticed by her friend, who is watching both of us with intense interest.

She glances at her watch and frowns.

"We got to get up there before he goes into his regularly scheduled 2 pm meeting."

"Right behind you."

I jog around my desk to catch up with her. We walk briskly down the corridor, clutching the files that contain the damning evidence and turning a few heads. I can't help but think about my father's reaction when he finds out about the scandal. He serves on both boards, and this revelation will undoubtedly send shockwaves through both companies. My anxiety builds as we take the elevator to the chairman's floor.

Taylor charges down the hall, ignoring the protests of his secretary, who insists that he's on an important call and we need to make an appointment. She barges into his office, looking as confident and in control as ever. I couldn't be prouder of her.

She's turning the tables on the boy's club she rightfully despises, and I get to witness it. If she forgives me for my earlier omission, I'd make her breakfast in bed and eat it off her delectable body.

"Mr. Williamson," Taylor begins, her voice strong and unwavering, "we've uncovered something that requires your immediate attention. It's about Jim Wraith and Roland Frasier. They've been embezzling."

"Let me call you back, Tom," Ted says quietly, his eyes never leaving Taylor's. Once he puts the phone in the cradle, he leans forward. "What did you just say?"

"Jim and Roland are embezzling," Taylor repeats as she approaches Ted's desk.

I clear my throat before backing up her claim.

"It's not just embezzlement, Ted. It's full-blown fraud, collusion, and conspiracy."

Ted's demeanor shifts immediately.

"Shut the door," he commands with a serious expression. "Explain."

I hand the files to Taylor and grasp the door as the secretary's eyes widen at the overheard statement. I place my index finger to my lips for her to keep quiet before closing us off from her startled expression.

Taylor's already laying out the documents in order of offense, weaving the evidence together in a pragmatic manner that makes it clear and concise. She dives into the details, explaining the fraudulent trades, the connections to the two executives and ending with the pictures, including the photo on her phone from the office Christmas party.

Ted interjects with questions, which she answers or defers to me. It's clear that he's taking the matter seriously but also grappling with the fraud happening right under his nose with his trusted CEO being intricately involved.

"Who discovered all this? Who took these pictures?" he demands, his gaze fixed on the documents across his desk. I step forward, answering before Taylor has a chance to.

"It was Taylor's idea to get the pictures to document the file, part of our due diligence. She was the one that put together the pieces and connected the dots."

Taylor interjects, "Paolo's being modest. It was his idea to conduct the site visits this morning. That broke it wide open and made it easy to come to the conclusion that we did."

Ted nods, seemingly satisfied with the response, though his expression remains troubled.

"This is a lot to take in. I'll need time to digest all of this. This stays strictly confidential until I meet with a few board members." He directs his attention to Paolo. "That includes keeping it from your father until I finish my investigation."

Our eyebrows go up when we exchange glances, which he immediately picks up. This is huge news, and I wouldn't dare have the secrets fall from my lips, and neither would Taylor.

"Oh, I suspected something," Ted says with a wry smile. His words hang in the air, and his eyes gleam with a knowing look as he continues, "That's why I left lunch abruptly. I had received news from an investigator I hired to shadow Roland."

The revelation hits me hard, causing my heart to race and my palms to sweat. Taylor gasps, and her hand instinctively covers her open mouth while her eyes fix on Ted.

"You two," he says with a meaningful pause, "make a formidable team. Good work."

Taylor recovers enough to murmur a thank you while I settle for a nod, acknowledging his compliment. I open the door for her and she breezes through as if nothing is amiss, even complimenting the secretary on her blouse. She excitedly grabs my arm when we round the corner, out of sight of everyone.

"We did it, Paolo. We exposed them."

Her green eyes shimmer with happiness and relief, replacing her intense expression throughout our meeting with Ted. At this moment, she looks so stunning that all my focus narrows to her lips, and an overwhelming desire to feel them on mine takes hold.

"How messed up is it that they are embezzling, and I'm happy we caught them? I mean, this could take down the whole company, and I could be out of a job," she says, shaking her head, her smile faltering when the elevator chimes.

She steps inside first, and when I cross the threshold, I wait for the doors to close and immediately hit the stop button. The elevator jerks to a halt, and her wide eyes turn to me.

"What are you doing?" she asks in a surprised voice.

"Taylor, before you go downstairs and return to being mad at me, I want to tell you how truly sorry I am for lying to you."

I step closer. The need to touch and hold her is overwhelming, and my fingers roll into fists to stop the craving.

"Paolo, you don't have to explain—"

"Yes, I do. I want you to know why I did it."

I take another step, her mouth closing, her eyes watching me curiously. She steps back, trying to keep the space between us respectable when I want to do very naughty things to her right here in this elevator.

"I dated someone older like you. I thought we'd be something, but I was wrong. She was promoted, and it included a transfer to a bigger market. I was happy for her and excited for this new chapter in our lives, but she didn't ask me to come along, and I easily would have."

I can see the understanding dawn in her eyes, a flicker of empathy that makes my confession easier to bear.

"When I heard your company's name, I knew it would be over. I knew it would be the end of something great, and I didn't want to feel that again. I know I messed up deciding for both of us and I hope you will forgive me for being so selfish."

She swallows hard, her gaze locked on mine. The attraction in the elevator is intense, and I can practically feel the heat radiating off her.

"That's why you made love to me," she murmurs, her eyes dropping to my lips for the first time in the elevator. I step forward, and she steps back, her body hitting the wall with nowhere to escape.

"Yes." My voice is barely above a whisper. "I didn't want you to think I was using you, and I wasn't sure I wanted it to end. I was so confused."

I caress her jawline with my knuckles as she drags in a ragged breath. Her skin feels like silk beneath my touch, and I can see the raw emotion in her eyes. The pull between us is undeniable, an intense connection that defies logic. Desire brought us together, but destiny will keep us together if only she agrees.

"But this week, working together, it's shown me that you're someone worth taking that kind of risk for. Taylor, I want to be with you, not just for the project but for more than that. Ted is right. We make a good team professionally, but personally too."

Her eyes search my face as I clasp her arms, my heart pounding with anticipation. Blood surges into my cock, straining against my pants and begging to be inside her, but now's not the right time. If she says yes, I'll spend all my free time making it up to her.

"I don't know, Paolo," she says hesitantly, her words laced with doubt. "With everything happening and the Jacobsen account still up in the air. Not to mention your father being on the board . . ." Her excuses sound flimsy even to her, and she notices the broad smile on my face. "Why are you looking at me like that?"

My hands slide over her skin, pulling her off the wall and embracing her in my arms. I whisper against her ear, "Those are the worst excuses from a big shot executive I've ever heard."

"Paolo," she protests, but I silence her with my lips.

Her full, soft lips mold to mine as she kisses me back with matched excitement. Her tongue traces the seam of my lips, begging for entry. I won't relent, teasing her with the tip of my tongue until she finally whimpers. I've wanted to do this all week, ever since I saw her in that black suit with matching stilettos strutting around those old men. If she only knew how many looked at her ass, the very one I'm grabbing right now, she'd be far more confident of her position and future at this company.

She drops her head back and moans as I bury my hands in her hair. Her neck is long and graceful, and I breathe in the sweet scent of her skin as I rain kisses down her throat.

"Tell me you want this, Taylor."

"Paolo..."

My name is a relieved sigh on her lips as she arches her back, inviting me to move lower to her chest. She fiddles with the button, the one from earlier that reminded me of the beautiful hickeys that adorn her skin.

"Tell me you want me as much as I want you."

I press my painfully hard cock into her soft body. She rocks her hips against me, her eyes falling closed as her fingers pull at my hair, drawing me toward those big breasts.

"Tell me that you are mine, and I'm yours."

I'm about to explode, holding myself back and waiting for her answer. I want to take her right now, mark her with more hickeys, and proclaim her as mine, but I need to hear her say it.

"I'm yours. Now fuck me, Paolo."

EPILOGUE

TAYLOR

"**Y**ou must be joking, Paolo. I'm not putting that on," I exclaim as I shake my hips, trying to get his erection out of my ass crack.

He doesn't move an inch, content to have me pressed against the countertop while tugging at my towel. I quickly spit my toothpaste into the sink and swish some water in my mouth.

"Agree, let's not wear anything and stay in eating candy off each other."

It was his idea to attend this Halloween party, so we're not backing out now. He tosses the black and red fabric strings comprising the lingerie onto the countertop beside me before grabbing my hips.

His playful expression and wiggling eyebrows make me chuckle when I glance at him in the mirror.

"That's not happening either. Or at least not yet."

He's too busy grinding himself against me to pay attention.

"You're getting yourself all riled up for nothing because we're going to the party. You just confirmed with your friend that we'd be there when he called a bit ago."

His chocolate eyes bore into mine as he stops grinding, grumbling in Italian long enough for me to straighten and face him. His arms tighten around my side, his hands kneading my ass while mine circle his neck.

"I know. I know, mia cara," he says with resignation. "I want you for myself. It's been a long week."

By *long week,* he means he hasn't had sex in three days.

Sad is the word he used to describe the first day we stayed late at the office. Mr. Williamson hired him full-time to help with the ongoing investigation, meaning he now has less free time than before. Combine that with the late nights and stress, and it's no wonder he's feeling a bit pent up.

On the other hand, I have been swamped with work as well, but I've had time to take care of my needs, something he wanted me to send videos of and I declined.

Tragic was the word he used the second day when he grabbed his dick in his dress pants while sitting in his office when we were supposed to discuss work. I had quarterly filings due, then a client dinner, and I met up with Chloe for drinks.

He happily wanted to crash, but I told him it was a girls' only night and I needed time with my best friend. He ended up working late and then went to play tennis with his friend Sebastian, who I'm meeting tonight.

Paolo preferred waiting before introducing me to his best friend. He mentioned something about not wanting to rush things and the possibility of his friend being a wealthy ladies' man who might steal me away. I chuckled and patted his chest to assure him that wasn't a possibility.

Dying was the word he used on the third day, which was yesterday. We're trying to keep a low profile at work, with the only person knowing we are involved being Chloe. She thinks it's funny to make faces and vulgar gestures when she catches us behind closed doors working. The all-glass offices prohibit public displays of affection, but we've been getting hot and heavy in the elevators.

Speaking of which, he didn't fuck me that day when he apologized, explains why he lied, and asked for another chance. The building security cut in, asking if we needed assistance or if the elevator had gotten stuck on its own.

Paolo sheepishly replied as I buttoned my blouse and got it started again. He did fuck me thoroughly that night and several times since until this recent dry spell. That was almost two weeks ago.

"When we return home, you can have your wicked way with me."

I roll onto the balls of my feet to kiss him when the hands cupping my ass scoop me up and carry me to his bed.

"Paolo, what are you doing?"

"Having my wicked way now," he murmurs, hovering over me with his usual excuse of air drying naked being better for his skin after showering. He's busy kissing my collarbones when my hand tangles into his hair.

"You smell so good."

"I smell like you."

His head darts up, casting me a playful smile as his lips dust mine once and then twice.

"I know."

When he starts to suck on my skin, my hand moves from his hair to his forehead, pushing it away from my skin with a slight pop to it.

"No hickeys, remember? You could if you hadn't picked out that ridiculous costume for me to wear."

It's actually really sweet.

I'm discovering that Paolo is far more sensitive than I initially thought. And when he insisted on taking pictures of us in our couple costumes for his travel blog, I thought it was a huge compliment. Although we were still trying to keep our

133

relationship a secret at work and didn't think the public pictures were a good idea, he pouted that lower lip, and I acquiesced.

"It's perfect for us. We're sleuths. Solving corporate fraud, one corrupt executive at a time," he jests, giving me a final kiss before lifting off me to finally get ready. "But tell me, Taylor. Are you corrupting me, or am I corrupting you?"

He raises an eyebrow while looking suspiciously at me along with his hard cock staring too. I laugh, accepting his hand to get off the bed and retrieve my costume from his bedroom door. As I grab the hanger, I feel a sense of contentment.

Despite the initial reservations and the glaring lie, I've found a connection with Paolo that I didn't anticipate when he first sat at the bakery. Something he confessed he had planned when he stood in line studying me. He said he knew right then and there that we would be great together. I don't believe him, but maybe he did.

I unfold the costumes, revealing a pair of Sherlock Holmes and Dr. Watson outfits. Considering our recent escapades in uncovering corporate fraud, Paolo's idea for our Halloween costumes is spot on. It's a clever and fitting choice.

And he's confident we'll win the best couple's costumes contest at the party, which includes year-long bragging rights and custom beer pong cups. A prize that's eluded him all these years. He told me that it was my responsibility to help him break his losing streak.

Turning to Paolo, I grin.

"Well, Sherlock, I suppose it's a bit of corruption on both sides."

His eyes light up with mischief as he watches me drag on the tight houndstooth dress with a pleated flared skirt.

"Indeed, my dear Watson. Let me corrupt you *before* the party."

The wide gold belt is barely buckled when his hands are suddenly everywhere, tugging the top down for my breasts to fall out and another hand diving under the skirt to rub my clit.

"You look so fucking hot that I can't help myself, mia cara." It comes out as a plea, a groan in his throat as his lips devour the side of my neck. "I must have you in this."

His fingers are no match for mine. Masturbating to thoughts of him is nothing compared to the real thing. I don't know why I didn't allow enough time to fuck each other's brains out after work and before this party. I was preoccupied with making an excellent first impression on his friends by being on time.

"Say yes, Taylor."

My head falls against his chest as my hand dives behind me to stroke his cock. His groan sounds more like a growl that rumbles through my back and makes me even more wet. His desire to have me as often as possible makes me feel wanted and attractive, something I never expected.

"Yes, Taylor," I mimic his words, accent and all before twirling in his arms and squatting low, making my intentions known.

"Fuck, yes."

His stance widens as I clench his stiff cock and swirl the pearl of cum around his head while his chocolate eyes stare down at mine. His fingers are already tugging the dress down so he has a better view of my breasts, which I think he's as addicted to as macarons.

He loves lingerie so long as it's demi bras that cup the breasts and don't cover the nipples. He loves to pluck, suck and bite them when he's not covering them in hickeys.

"You're obsessed."

"Yes."

I roll my eyes before inching closer to latch onto his cock. A shudder runs through him as I work my tongue over his foreskin. The sensitivity of being uncut gets him every time.

"Taylor." The usual roll of the 'r' is impatient as I lick and tease the delicate skin, something he loves to hate. "Be a good girl and suck me off properly."

"Mmm."

I love it when he says that. It makes my pussy clench in anticipation, and a wave of heat wash over me. It's the combination of praise and power over him mixed with him being younger and stronger. It's a tantalizing mind fuck that gets me turned on.

"Like this?"

I cup his balls, rolling them in my hand as I flatten my tongue against the side of his cock for long sweeping strokes. It's precisely the opposite of what he wants, something I've learned very quickly as he loves giving and receiving oral sex.

Where I want to savor every inch of him in my mouth, he wants it hard and fast, spurting down my throat in minutes so he can fuck me for a longer time.

He's a fast comer the first time and then takes forever the multiple times after. I love it. I'm guaranteed countless orgasms as he can hold out for almost an hour before releasing. It makes for long, hot, sweaty sex sessions and lazy Sundays spent mostly in bed.

Growing unsatisfied, he weaves his long, thin fingers into my hair and moves my head where he wants. His hand holds his cock at my mouth, tapping it against my lips as I smile.

"You're such a tease."

"It doesn't always have to be fast and in a hurry," I chide, knowing damn well he's never in a hurry to have sex.

He wants it all the time for a very long time. The blowjobs or eating me out is always a precursor to sex. It's never just the only sex act—another thing I enjoy with him.

"I want to come," he complains, stroking his cock as I lick the tip. It's a playful negotiation I enjoy drawing out even though we're already late.

"Come. I'm not stopping you. You can even come on my chest if you want."

Knowing he loves that too, but he won't. He's too far gone, envisioning me on my knees in this costume blowing him.

"Taylor."

His hips thrust forward, ending all teasing and discussion as his hard cock pushes past my lips. Knowing exactly how he likes it and loving that I'm the only one that gets to do this to him, I replace his hand when it falls away and pump and suck him.

It's fast and sloppy, saliva dripping down my chin as his fingertips gently cup my head and the feverous pace I'm setting. His other hand twists and pinches my nipple, making me so damn horny that I can't wait to be fucked.

Enough teasing him. I need to get him off so I can get off. I'm so ready to be fucked into oblivion by that young, hard cock that I can feel my wetness clinging to my inner thighs.

When his balls tighten and his fingers hold my head closer to his cock, I know he's on the verge of spilling into my mouth. My tongue works overtime, swirling as I pump his shaft and pull groans and moans out of him.

"*Mia cara*," he slurs, sending a hot string of cum onto my tongue and down my throat.

His clean diet and love of pineapple juice are evident in how good he tastes. Something that is surprisingly important to him. I stare up at him as he finishes. His head tilts toward the ceiling and his eyes slide close.

The expression is one of relief, contentment, and happiness. Something I will never tire of seeing. When his hips are still, his eyes open to gaze down at me with a renewed intensity.

"You look stunning with my cock down your throat."

His fingers lift from my head, as do those at my nipple, while said cock slips from my mouth. He helps me to my feet, my mouth ringed with saliva and remnants of cum that he wipes away with the towel I tossed on the bed.

"You always say that, but am I stunning with it not down my throat?"

I'm kidding. He's always overflowing with compliments, more so than my ex ever did. It's definitely a love language of his and one I'm loving now that I'm experiencing it.

"You are stunning in every way." His lips dip to mine, yielding the softest, most sincere kiss ever. It lasts only a moment before he stands straight. "Especially this way."

His hands hold my waist tightly as he turns me around, making his intentions clear. It's my turn, and I couldn't be more ready to be fucked hard and fast. I need to get off as desperately as he did a second ago.

"Fuck me, Paolo."

I clutch the bed frame, shoving my ass into his hard dick before he sheathes it. His hands pull on my hips, lining me up with him and flipping the skirt to expose my warm skin to the cold room.

His hand moves from my hip to the back of my belt, using it to hold me in place. It's sexy as he slides in slowly, inch by inch, opening me wider and wider until I'm full. I let out a contented sigh, relishing this feeling as he slips out equally slowly.

"Who's teasing who now?" I ask, glancing over my shoulder as he watches his erection slide slowly back into me.

When his eyes flicker to mine, a soft smile pulls at his lips before he returns to watching himself. He looks lost in the moment, utterly enjoying the view and me and us. As I turn around, I arch into him and succumb to the intentionally slow movements of his sensual body. If he wants to fuck me slowly, so be it.

Aside from our breathy sounds occasionally falling in unison, the room is quiet. His fingers on the belt lighten with his slower pace as he adjusts his angle to hit near my favorite spot. The tiniest ember of orgasm builds deep within me, and I close my eyes to concentrate on our connected bodies.

To focus on the fullness and the emptiness, the ebb and flow of my desire as he gives me what I want and then takes it away. My head droops, and my shoulders relax, inviting his hand to caress the exposed skin.

He rattles off something in Italian, which is far too long and complicated to ask him to translate but adds to our intimacy. I see his expression when he brushes my hair over my shoulder and catches my chin to look back at him. It's soft and humble, obviously as affected by this lovemaking as I am. His eyes glimmer with affection as his finger caresses my cheek.

"It means I care for you deeply."

Suddenly, we're too far away.

Not close enough for those sweet words to spill from his mouth. I straighten, which ejects him from my pussy only long enough for me to capture his hand, lead him to the bed where I lay on my back, and invite him to lay with me. He crawls on top, slides back in, and hovers over me with a questionable look.

"I wanted to be closer, so I can do this."

I lean up, capture his lips, and pull him entirely over me. Buried under his long, lean body as he slowly makes love to me, the same as when he lied. Although, this time, I know it's not a lie. His feelings are in every hidden glance, stolen kiss, and intentional touch.

He kisses me long and deep, thoroughly and expertly as if pouring his emotion into his tongue, mouth, and body. My pussy clenches in the slowest, most sensual orgasm to overcome me when he breaks for air. The same gentle smile he had on his face when I met him at the bakery adorns it now.

As his silky hair falls forward, I brush it behind his ear and say, "I care deeply for you too, Paolo."

**Turn the page to read Chapter One of
Sebastian and Chloe's story!**

SEBASTIAN: CHAPTER 1
SEBASTIAN AND CHLOE'S STORY

I'm jolted awake by a searing headache, a brutal reminder of last night when I closed down a bar in Midtown. I almost got laid but struck out in the ninth inning. I'd been chatting with this tiny hot chick, hitting it off in the kind of way you do in dimly lit bars with music blaring, but then her friend decided to hurl.

My chivalrous side kicked into overdrive, and I offered up my driver to ensure they made it home safely. In my not-so-sober state, it seemed like a brilliant plan to invite her to my place for an after-hours party once her friend was handled. Now, in the unforgiving morning light and with a clearer head, I can't help but cringe at how sketchy it all sounds. It gives off a major creeper vibe.

The room spins when I force my eyes open. Little sledge-hammers are pounding inside my skull as I lay sprawled across my bed, gazing at the masterpiece on the ceiling. Bathed in the soft, golden glow of the chandelier, this mural is a vibrant display of Italian mythology and history, set against a backdrop of cerulean blue.

In one corner, Apollo, the sun god, rides his chariot across the sky, and it feels like he's casting beams of light that dance with every flicker of the chandelier. Nearby, Venus rises from the foamy waves, her beauty and grace captivating. The entire ceiling is a tribute to Italy's rich cultural heritage, blending figures from Dante's Divine Comedy, Botticelli's Birth of Venus, and Michelangelo's Creation of Adam into a harmonious tapestry.

It's not my style, but then again, this was my parents' bedroom when the artists were commissioned and flown in from Florence. This entire home is a shrine to them, frozen in time since they passed away. It's as if I'm living in one of the famed museums in Italy with the watchful gaze of my dead ancestors on the walls, silently judging my every move. If I were smart, I would have moved out of this haunted house and let the new owners deal with the ghosts that linger from my past. Instead, I chose to stay stuck in a life I have no idea how to traverse, chained to a past I no longer wanted.

A light tapping on the door draws my attention to Jiles, my parent's loyal house manager, standing in the doorway with clasped hands and a warm smile.

"Good morning, Mr. Sebastian," he greets me in his impeccable British accent.

Something Mamma had insisted on when they sold their interests in Milan to launch their empire in Houston—a British butler. Mamma had studied in London and had been fascinated with the British monarchy. She wanted to replicate the life and lifestyle here when she hired Jiles before I was born. In actuality, he's far more than a house manager. He's my friend, caregiver, and a father figure.

"Ugh, what time is it?" I grumble as he enters the room to press the button for the floor-to-ceiling drapes covering the wall of windows that overlook the back terrace.

Jiles checks his pocket watch, a vintage piece that has been in his family for generations.

"After 1 pm."

Damn, it's late.

With great effort, I battle my body to sit up in bed, and the room spins faster. My disheveled hair clings stubbornly to one side, tangled and unruly. The air in the room stinks from the acrid scent of my breath—the alcohol reminiscent of gasoline fumes. I'm still clad in my shirt from last night, my pants are tossed across the bed, and my shoes are strewn about my floor. The room is suddenly flooded with blinding light, and I can't help but curse at the invasion.

"Damn, Jiles, could you close those curtains? It's like staring at the gates of Heaven," I complain and throw my hand over my eyes to block the assault. He chuckles at my misery.

"Perhaps a strong coffee and a hot shower to start the day?"

Always the voice of reason, he disappears into the bathroom without awaiting my reply. Once I hear the water flowing, I drop my hand and allow my eyes to adjust to the scene that stretches before me outside my windows.

The terrace has undergone a magical metamorphosis, resembling a pristine white winter wonderland. My best buddy, Paolo, and I had discussed themes like my parents always did for their charity parties. Since this is the first that I am hosting since their passing years ago, he suggested I pick a favorite theme from one of their old parties. Thus, a winter wonderland was born.

Tons of pristine white blow-in snow blankets the ground, shimmering under the sun's golden rays. The weather gods in Texas decided to bless us with an early cold front, which will ensure the snow doesn't melt in the usually humid Houston sun. Fake icicles glisten from the eaves and tree branches, and white lights adorn everything the eye can see.

Dozens of white-flocked Christmas trees with commemorative ornaments that guests will take later are scattered throughout the property. In the center of it all stands a magnificent Christmas tree with hundreds of wrapped gifts around it, ready for the children to arrive.

Instead of boat rides in the large pool, I contracted a small ice rink to be set up over it, where children can skate with their parents. Lit white garland, wreaths, and snowflakes adorn every railing, doorway, and available surface. Lanterns light the stairs to the pavilion as different vendors and staff members bustle around the grounds.

When contemplating themes with Paolo, I was embarrassed that I couldn't remember the more recent ones, having been too drunk at the time. Hearing my antics played back to me as we looked through the photo albums was something I wasn't proud of. That's why I decided to break away from the upscale, high-society parties my parents used to host—where women wore beaded gowns, men donned tuxedos, and fur coats collected by the dozens in coat check.

I knew I couldn't live up to the glitz and glamour of my parents's legacy charity events. The thought of inviting a bunch of rich old people to reminisce about memories of my parents all night sounded too depressing and wasn't something I could stomach.

Instead, I went in a different direction and made it all about the kids. Instead of having the firefighters pick up the gifts to deliver to the children days later, I contacted the organization, requested copies of the children's wish lists, and invited the children and their families to my party.

It was a decision that resonated with me on a deep level. My parents had always been known for their generosity and instilled in me the importance of giving back to those in need. What better way to honor their memory than by creating an event that would bring smiles to the faces of children who deserved a magical Christmas?

As I watched the staff and vendors working tirelessly to transform my estate into a winter wonderland, I felt a sense of purpose and fulfillment I hadn't experienced in a long time. The thought of making a difference in these children's lives, even for just a day, filled me with a warmth far more comforting than any fur coat chucked in a coat check.

"Mr. Sebastian? Did you hear me?" Jiles repeats while moving into my line of vision. I shake my head, clearing away the justifications I always have with myself when breaking from the shadows of my parents' former glory.

"Sorry, what?"

I rub my temples, knowing a bloody Mary would help more than a shower and coffee, but Jiles would never let me continue drinking to alleviate one of my hangovers. And I won't be drunk at my party. At least not until the children leave.

"Your shower is ready. Ms. Martha has your breakfast ready. Do you want to eat up here or in the breakfast room? As you may recall, the dining room is the staging area for the Miracle on Sugar Street candy station."

That was my idea. I loved candy growing up, and my parents restricted it. To enter, the children will walk through a life-sized gingerbread house where elves will take their family picture against a North Pole backdrop. Holiday music will be piped through the property as they are offered hot chocolate with whipped cream and peppermint stirs on their way inside the sweet candy shop.

The kids can select from glass displays of candies and treats, glass jars filled with gumballs and jawbreakers, and decorative containers with chocolates and pralines while the parents enjoy croissants and coffee. Paolo even recommended the bakery where he met his girlfriend to cater it.

"I'll eat downstairs. Any chance I can get a bloody Mary?"

I wiggle my eyebrows and then groan at the action. It's far too much movement with this splitting headache.

"No," Jiles says firmly, gathering my pants and shoes from the room and disappearing into my dressing closet.

"I didn't think so," I grumble, gritting my teeth as I slip from the bed to gingerly walk into the large bathroom with steam billowing from the top of the shower. It's a terrible mistake that I don't keep alcohol in here. It would be perfect to take a nip with the aspirin that I'm hunting through the medicine cabinet to find.

"Don't take too long. Mr. Paolo is on his way over," Jiles calls from the other room.

I mutter under my breath, aware that he can't hear me as I swallow the pills dry, shed last night's attire that reeks of a brewery, and step into the steamy water. The hot stream soothes my aching body, providing a momentary escape from last night's indulgences. With each passing minute of it beating down on my stiff muscles, I start to wake up and begin to feel more like myself.

I rush through the rest of my shower routine, dry off, and wrap a plush towel around my waist. Deciding to postpone shaving, I opt for comfortable clothes and reserve the whole getting-ready process for later this afternoon. That's when I'll don my custom-made Santa suit—a tradition passed down from Papa. He dressed like Father Christmas and brought us presents after midnight mass on Christmas Eve when I was a kid.

As I descend the stairs to the first floor, I can't help but be overwhelmed by the sheer beauty of the grand foyer, adorned with all of Mamma's meticulously chosen decorations. Jiles had taken great care in preserving her sense of style, documenting everything for the estate and backing it up with photographs.

I used to scoff at their organized excessiveness but now, seeing everything precisely as she would have decorated it, I'm struck with nostalgic happiness and profound loneliness. It's why I haven't decorated the house in years—it brings up too many memories. Doing it for the children chases away some of the heartbreak.

When my feet hit the bottom step, Paolo's striding through the double doors, letting out a low whistle as his eyes roam the foyer.

"Seb, this place looks incredible! Your mamma really had an eye for decorations."

Paolo's dressed casually, looking like he's just come from the gym or something. I'd ask him to play tennis if I didn't have this damn hangover and the courts weren't already crowded with bouncy houses and other kid activities.

"Yeah, she did. Jiles made sure everything was decorated the way she would have liked it." I clap him on the back to take it all in and feel a bittersweet pride.

Paolo's eyes light up as they land on a child-sized toy train, positioned as if ready for one of the kids coming tonight to hop on for a ride.

"Hey, isn't that the toy train we used to fight over, taking turns riding it around your house when we were kids?"

I chuckle at the memory. How Jiles managed to keep it running year after year was a mystery.

"You mean the same train that miraculously survived our epic fistfights over who got to ride it first? Yeah, that's the one."

Paolo grins, clearly feeling as nostalgic as I am. I can't blame him. This time of year brings it out in everyone.

"I thought for sure we destroyed it that one year when you tackled me and sent me flying into the marble column in the kitchen. Your papa asked if there was a doctor in the house. Because of the ball, so many were in attendance that they argued over who was more qualified to set my broken arm."

I throw my head back and laugh while gripping his shoulder even tighter. Paolo has always been tall and lanky, while I, thanks to Mamma's side of the family, carried more bulk on my frame. He was a scrawny kid who usually got the short end of the stick when we wrestled.

"I forgot all about that. You were walling like a baby. What were we? Seven or eight?"

"You broke my arm. Of course, I was crying. And we were *twelve*. The reason why I know this is because I missed my chance of playing at Cooperstown after my father pulled all those strings to get me on the team even though I was living back home in Milan at the time," The dejection still rings in his words as if it had just happened. I give him a good shake before releasing him.

"Tell ya what, I can pull some strings and get you a private lesson with a guy on the Yankees. Will that make up for it?"

"And this is why you don't understand team sports."

He shakes his head and walks over to one of the trees, his fingertips sending an ornament twirling as it hangs from the branch. I join him, standing off to the side as he continues touching various decorations as if recalling his own memories.

"Man, we were something else back then, weren't we?"

I nod, feeling grateful that my childhood friend is still my family.

"Yeah, we were."

The memories, as wonderful as they are, only intensify the loneliness in my chest. I rub it absentmindedly, a dull ache reminding me of the void left behind by my parents.

**Read the rest of Sebastian and Chloe's story in *Sebastian*
(The Cougars and Cubs Series 💋, Book 2)**

When Santa Claus IS the gift this holiday season.

In the glittering world of Houston's elite, Chloe Miller, a driven financial analyst with an unbreakable spirit, stands out not for her wealth but for her impeccable fashion sense. Yet behind the façade of success lies a childhood shadowed by poverty, where Christmas was a harsh reminder of what she couldn't afford. Her desire for glamour and a better life led her to build a fortress of designer clothes and accessories, guarding her against the judgment of a world that had once looked down on her. When an invitation to the high-society charity Christmas party hosted by the charismatic heir to immense wealth, Sebastian Agnelli, arrives, Chloe's skepticism mingles with her fear of being judged for her humble beginnings.

Sebastian Agnelli, a playboy with a flamboyant lifestyle, longs for something more meaningful. Haunted by the painful loss of his parents in a plane crash during his college years, he is burdened by wealth he never wanted. Their fateful encounter at the charity event becomes the spark that sets their worlds on a collision course.

As the holiday season unfolds, their connection deepens, and the walls they've built around their hearts start to crumble. Chloe's fear of judgment and Sebastian's need for authenticity form a potent mix, challenging them to confront their pasts and insecurities.

As the magic of the holiday season envelops them, Chloe and Sebastian navigate the complexities of love, trust, and transformation. Can they move beyond their fears and pasts to build a future together, defined not by wealth but by the power of authenticity and love?

Sebastian is a heartwarming tale of romance, redemption, and the enchantment of the holiday spirit, where two individuals find that the most precious gifts can't be bought with wealth but are discovered in the depths of the heart.

Sebastian is the second book in The Cougars and Cubs Series 💋 and is a connected standalone. It is a steamy, reverse age-gap, opposites attract, holiday romance.

GET A FREE BOOK

Sign up for my newsletter to ensure you are the first to know about new releases, sneak peek excerpts, cover reveals, book sales, and author giveaways!

The Cañon Series 🖤
is deliciously dark and intensely traumatic.

DOWNLOAD FOR FREE ON MY WEBSITE
www.gigimeier.com

Dani and Tomlin's story is a single POV, slow burn, enemies-to-lovers, forced proximity romance. Check my website for a list of content and trigger warnings.

BONUS CONTENT

Want more?

I have exclusive bonus and deleted scenes for you on my website: www.gigimeier.com/freebies.

I'm always adding more for my loyal readers as a big THANK YOU for loving my books and supporting me as an author 🤍

IF YOU ENJOYED THIS BOOK

Thank you for reading *Paolo,* the first book in The Cougars and Cubs Series 🍂 . Stick around for *Sebastian*, the second book in the series and a Christmas romance.

If you enjoyed *Paolo,* please consider leaving a review on BookBub, Goodreads, or your favorite retailer to let others know about this steamy, reverse age gap, meet cute, autumn themed, workplace romance.

Reviews are greatly appreciated. They help independent authors like myself get our books in front of more readers.

Gigi Meier

ALSO BY GIGI MEIER

Standalone Book

Coyote

Sammie and Carlos's forced proximity

cartel, kidnapped, Military hero, dark romance

The Cañon Series

Tomlin

The start of Dani and Tomlin's

slow burn, enemies-to-almost-lovers

Tomlin Takahashi Duet #1

The Cañon Series, Book #1

Takahashi

The conclusion of Dani and Tomlin's

friends-to-lovers, happily ever after

Tomlin Takahashi Duet #2

The Cañon Series, Book #2

Hamilton

Hamilton and Molli's second chance,

small town, police officer romance

The Cañon Series, Book #3

Isla

Isla and Gabe's opposites attract,

age gap, forbidden love romance

The Cañon Series, Book #4

The Cougars and Cubs Series 💋

Paolo

Taylor and Paolo's reverse age gap,

forced proximity, office romance

The Cougars and Cubs Series 💋, Book #1

Sebastian

Sebastian and Chloe's reverse age gap,

opposites attract, Christmas romance

The Cougars and Cubs Series 💋, Book #2

Giovanni

Giovanni and Kacie's reverse age gap,

protector, Alpha male romance

The Cougars and Cubs Series 💋, Book #3

Kadus

Kadus and Bex's reverse age gap,

best friend's brother, rockstar romance

The Cougars and Cubs Series 💋, Book #4

Marco

Marco and Victoria's reverse age gap,

steamy Latin couple, soulmates romance

The Cougars and Cubs Series 💋, Book #5

Gods and Goddesses Anthology

Eternal Reign

Hades and Persephone Modern Retelling

Russian bratva, kidnapping, touch her and die, slow burn.

ABOUT THE AUTHOR

After retiring from a thirty-year career in corporate America, GiGi Meier is delighted to be writing romance novels about strong female characters and their complicated, swoon-worthy men.

She loves telling stories and figuring out why her characters do what they do. With heartbreaking angst, panty-dropping lust, and enviable love, her stories linger long after you close the book.

When GiGi is not eating over her laptop, she likes to spend time in the pool with her children, walk her furry babies, and film videos for Instagram and YouTube. Whether attending a book club or hosting a game night, she loves connecting with new people and making friends.

Sign up for my newsletter to ensure you are the first to know about new releases, sneak peek excerpts, cover reveals, book sales, and author giveaways!

www.gigimeier.com